Gangsta Killers

"The Betrayal"

Also by Veronica Meek

The Hitman Daugther's

Peek-A-Boo

Gangsta Killers

"The Betrayal"

Veronica Meek

Writer's Block Publications
P.O. Box 640
Jonesboro, GA 30237

ISBN-13: 978-0615792750

ISBN-10: 0615792758

Cover Design by: The Lyricist Firm

Edited by: Kiara Reynolds

Manufactured in the United States of America

ACKNOWLEDGEMENTS

First, I like to thank God for all the love I have received. He has grace me with so much and he would never know how graceful that I am.

Second, I like to thank my mother and father they have stood beside me the whole way and I don't know how I would ever be able to thank you.

Third, I like to thank my kids: Devonta, Tamaya, and Tynisha for being just as supporting and giving me that push that I need.

Fourth I like to thank my brother's Samuel and Brian along with my sisters Tacora and Brianna for helping me out whenever you can. I would also like to show love to my family and to also say thank you for being there for me.

Last, but not least I like to say thank you to Lynnett Fox, Troy Black, John Ramos, and Mike Sudlers for being there and helping me get this far, and to let you know that I will always be a Firm Diva and apart of The Lyricist Firm for life.

"Gangsta Killer"

I started off as one of the best marksmen.

I ended up in total darkness.

I woke up alone, afraid and scared.

What I didn't know I was one of the worse feared.

I took one bullet to the head in December.

When I woke up I couldn't even remember.

That I was one hell of a

Gangsta Killer.

Chapter 1

Mike

When I open my eyes pain shoots from the front all the way down to the back of my head. It's takes a moment for my sight to begin to clear. I look around trying to figure out where I am, but the only thing I see is a big bay window. When I looked out; all I see is rain hitting heavily on the window pane.

The room is dark; the only light is coming from the street lights below. I try to listen for a sound, any sound, but all I hear is the sound of the pouring rain.

I close my eyes again hoping that something will come back to me, but everything is foggy. I can't remember anything at all so I begin to panic, and for the life of me I don't know why. Why am I so scared? Why am I here in this cold dark place? I can't help but ask myself this question over and over again, but I still don't have an answer. It is clear to see that I am lying inside a hospital room.

I look down hoping to see a name tag or something that can at least tell me who I am. I try to move my hands and hear a clinking sound. That's when I notice I am bound to the bedrails.

Now panic really sets in. Why am I handcuffed to the bed? What could I have done for me to end up like this? My heart starts to race and the monitors begin to sound off. Oh God, am I having a heart attack? It sure feels like it. Sweat begins to pour from my body as my head begins to pound.

My room door flies open as doctors and nurses come running inside, and there are people everywhere. Some are pushing buttons on the machines while others try working on me. I'm not able to speak, but I can hear them asking me questions.

"Mr. Crawford you need to calm down." The doctor says while leaning over me.

If I could calm down don't they know I would have done so by now? My chest is killing me. Oh God I'm dying. I know I am.

"Mr. Crawford I'm going to ask you some questions. Please try to answer if you can. It's very important. Do you understand me?"

I try to reply, but I'm still not able to get any words out; so I nod my head "yes."

"Good. Now listen to me Mr. Crawford; I really need you to try and calm down. Everything is going to be alright. You need to get your emotions under control. I know it is scary waking up and not knowing where you are. But you have to believe me we're only here to help you."

I try to lift my hands up so I can show her I'm handcuffed to the bed.

She looks down. "Oh, that was for your safety Mr. Crawford. You kept pulling out your IV's, but now that you're awake we can remove them. You see that you've been here for a while but I want to know if you remember what happened to you."

Since I only have one means of communication I shake my head no. I am more confused now than when I first opened my eyes.

"I'm going to explain things as best as I can."

Believe me. I am more than ready to know what happened to me and why I am here. There's one good thing that came from having this attack; and that is that I learn my last name.

"I'm going to start from the beginning. On November 23, you were brought here for multiple gunshots to your chests and you were shot once in the head. You are a very lucky young man. Tell me Mr. Crawford, do you remember anything about that day or what happened to you?"

"No!" I even surprise myself when I answer her question.

"Do you know your whole name?"

"No I don't doctor. I can't remember a damn thing." I say angrily.

"It's okay Mr. Crawford. That's a normal reaction for someone that has brain trauma. The good news is that most of the swelling is gone, but you still have a long way to go."

"How long have I been here?" My voice sounds as weak as I feel.

"You have been here a little over two months."

"Two months!"

I watch the doctor sit down on the edge of the bed. She lifts my hands up and removes the cuffs. When she looks down at me she smiles. It helps me to relax a little more. The shock I am in is all but gone except for the headache, which is pounding like a drum. She has a way of making a man forget everything, even the pain that is pounding in my head.

"Would you like something for the pain? I notice you keep rubbing the side of your head."

"Yes I would love something thank you. Can you answer something else for me doctor?"

"Sure. What is it?"

"What is my first name?" I tried to smile but the pain is unbearable.

"It's Mike, but that is enough for today. I'm going to leave you to get some more rest. Someone will be back to give you something for the pain. Tomorrow we'll have a lot to talk about before I call the police and let them know that you're awake."

"Thank you doctor, this means a lot to me and maybe by then I will have remembered more about what happened to me."

"Mike, you do not need to rush your memory; it will come back in time. Rushing it will only cause more headaches. Just relax and get some sleep."

"I think I been sleeping long enough Doctor."

"Yes, but the more you rest and sleep, the better your chances of healing and getting your memory back."

I close my eyes when she turned to walk away. I didn't even bother to open them when I heard the door open and close again. I heard someone moving around getting what they needed together.

"Mr. Crawford, we'll have you feeling better in no time." The person said.

Whatever she gave me, put me out in minutes. I didn't even hear her when she left the room.

Cory

I treat today like any other day. I make my rounds, check my supplies, and make my way to see my big brother. The months seem to move slowly waiting on Mike to wake up. But believe me, I am more than happy to receive the phone call informing me that Mike has woken from his coma.

I know that my brother is lucky to be alive, and I've prayed to God every day that he would save him even though he has taken so many lives himself. The work we do is deadly and Mike paid the price for slipping. It damn near ended his life.

I do not know what I would do if I lost one of my brothers, because it has always been the three of us. No one looked after Isaiah and I, like Mike has and now it's our time to return the favor. Since the day he was shot, I had my ear to the street trying to find out who was responsible. Lately, I've felt like I'm very close to figuring it out, but only Mike can tell me the truth.

I hated watching him waste away in that hospital bed. He was nothing but skin and bones now; it wasn't like he was a very big man just tall.　　When　　people looked at him they saw power and they knew right off that he was the one to turn too when you needed a job done.

Isaiah and I learned from the best; no one could ever take his place. It was like watching one of the mighty God's fall.

I look over at my ole girl sitting next to me in the car. She wants nothing more than for me to step into Mike's shoes. Jamaya doesn't understand the bond my brother's and I have and I had to listen to her go on and on about who should be the one running our family now that Mike's hurt, but there was one head of this family and that's Mike. How can I get her to understand that? It's like whatever I say goes in one ear and out the other. The bitch is just money hungry; I knew that and always have since day one.

There is one thing I can say about Jamaya, and that is she's a ride and die chick. No matter how money hungry she is she has always had my back; from the beginning until now. I hate to let her down, but Mike is our boss and she has to understand that.

"Cory, do you know how long Mike's been awake?" Jamaya asked.

"No, and I do not care as long as he's awake. Now I will be able to look into my bro face and finally get some answers."

"Yeah." Jamaya said as she rolled her eyes. "Thanks to you he will be able to walk right back in on top. I told your ass to step up and take what you want and now it's too late."

Before I knew what happened I had her by the neck pulling her from her seat sideways.

With my face close to hers I stressed. "Jamaya I telling you this for the last fucking time Mike is the head of this family. Do not make me have to say this shit again, because to be honest with you this is getting tiresome."

I've never seen her cry before; it surprised me when her eyes start to fill with tears. I hate hurting her so it made my grip loosen.

"Why do you always do this baby? You always make me hurt you."

It was hard to let her go; sometimes she pushed all the wrong buttons. She tried to smile, but was shaken badly. I could tell she wasn't happy that I still hadn't let her go. Sometimes she made me want to kill her. I don't release her until my cell phone starts to ring. I heard her butt hit the car seat as she tried to pull in some much needed air.

"Speak. Yeah I'm on my way now thanks for the update Doc."

Once again I find myself looking over at Jamaya. She is trying not to look at me, because she has tears rolling down her face.

"Baby come here." I pull her by the arm to move her closer to me. She doesn't even try to resist. "I'm sorry baby you know I do not like hurting you, but you don't know when to stop. This is my bro you keep talking about. I would not be a man if I continued to let you disrespect him like that. You feel me?"

I can feel her head shaking yes on my chest. I know then. I have finally got my message across. Why did it have to take all that for her to understand the loyalty between me and my brothers? Why do I have to damn near beat it through her head?

"Baby I love you; you know that so please stop crying."

"I love you too baby; I'm sorry. I always find ways of pissing you off." She says sniffling.

"Yeah that you do." I laugh. "I do not have a right to put my hands on you though." I kiss her softly on her forehead. Since I am feeling sorry for her, I let her lay there a few seconds more. She feels good in my arms. This is one of the moments when I hate to let her go. "Okay baby. Now we have to get to the hospital."

Silence fills the car most of the way to South Side Hospital. When I look over at Jamaya this time I see that she is busy fixing her makeup. I know then that she has put her brick wall back up. She hates to show signs of weakness, but mostly I do too. I reach down and push the play button on my CD player. It wasn't long before Gucci Mane's voice fills the car.

Once she is done with her makeup she reaches over and picks up her matching pair of Dolce Gabbana sunglasses. Heading down Upper Riverdale Road this time, it feels different, though I have taken this same route so many times before. This time it seems a lot easier.

Isaiah

As soon as I pull the trigger blood flies on my brand new pair of Jordan's. Damn, I hate messing up my shit, because I never know when I'll have somewhere else to go. Like today I'm heading to see my brother and this fool just leaked all over me. Maybe I need to start wrapping plastic bags around my shoes; or I should go as far as putting on a jump suit in that case. I laugh to myself.

The sound of moaning brings me back to reality. I look down and this fool is fighting death the whole way. What I need to do? Damn near blow his head off?

"Fool just die!" I say aloud.

He looks up at me with glazed eyes. I saw that he is hanging on with as much life as I have in my little finger. I give him credit; he is really putting up a fight. He's holding on to every last minute.

"Damn fool." I say aloud as I point the gun and shoot once more.

I saw the look he gave me right before I pull the trigger; I guess he hoped that I might have had some kind of heart. What he doesn't know is that I'm as heartless as they come. Sometimes I believe I'm the worst out of the three of us. Don't get me wrong. I don't mind or care about being a cold hearted killer. It's in my blood; it's part of my nature. If my brothers were not walking this earth I would not give a damn about nobody.

I look down at my shoes again and head to my truck shaking my head. Lucky for me, I just went and grabbed another pair from Greenbrier this morning. I hit the button and the locks sound off in the quiet neighborhood. I looked around knowing there has to be a bag somewhere in here to put these shoes in. As soon as I see it, I pull it out, and slide out of my shoes. My feet hit the cold ground and a chill goes right up my spine.

I pull out my new pair of J's and ease my foot inside; grabbing the box and gas can I walked back over to the body. This is the part of the job I hate. I should just leave this nigga right here. I hate the smell of a burning body. When I open up the gas can and started to pour the smell of gas was strong. I took a second and pulled out the matches. After striking it I dropped it down on the body. In a matter of seconds the body goes up in flames. I take the box with the shoes inside and added it to the growing flames. Just for good measure I pour a little more gas to keep the fire burning hot.

The flames are sky high now; the best part about my surroundings is that not one soul can see it. I stand there watching as the flames dance across the empty buildings. I watched as the fire burns until there is nothing left. It didn't take that long he isn't much bigger than a ten year old boy. That's what Rico gets for trusting a small as man. They ain't shit.

Mike has always told us never trust a man if he isn't at least 5'7. The smaller they are the sneakier they are. For some reason those hard legs just want learn. That's that reason they sent people like me and my brother's after them.

Our circle is small and only the best is allowed to do what we do; we better not even get word of someone else around here doing hits in Atlanta. That's our department. If they want to continue to pull air through their lungs they best to find another business.

I hear sounds of dogs in the background. It isn't good to hang around the crime scene for too long. I don't care how far away from the city it is. My mind goes back to Mike and my heart freezes over again. I just can't believe we almost lost him; the streets are lucky we didn't, because that would have opened up the gates of hell.

I feel myself getting angry about the whole situation again. I really need to learn how to control the anger I have inside of me. First, of all it isn't good for business; it damn sure isn't good for me. But I have always been a hot head. That's what Mike always calls me. It puts a smile on my face, because I know the first thing he's going to say as soon as he sees me···"I know you haven't been out there being a hot head Isaiah."

No one knows me better than him, so there's not going to be a reason to lie. It's who I am; nothing's going to change that.

My drive back to the city does wonders for me. I am at ease; nearly at peace with myself, and that's a good thing. Mike knows when I'm on some crazy shit.

With me being in the middle of Mike and Cory it's like I have to work even harder to please both of them. They both seem to have their own things going on, and I'm left to keep the peace. It just surprised me that Cory hasn't tried to step up and take Mike's place. It's been plenty of times I've overheard that no good as bitch of his in his ear trying to full his head with it. I told that boy Jamaya ain't know good, but when you're in love you don't hear anything anyone trying to tell you.

I'm not going to keep thinking about that; it isn't going to do nothing but stress me right back out. I don't need that. I can't wait to see my bro man it seems like forever since I looked in his eyes.

With that in mind I floored it. I know I'm pushing the speed limits, but today is a good day; tickets be damn. I pass car after car pushing my Yukon to the limit. Even going ninety miles she still rides smooth as hell. I love this truck. I fly in and out of traffic blowing my horn driving like a mad man. I finally feel my blood start to warm from the excitement of the ride. I finally feel a little human. That's what I live for, the thrill of the chase.

*C*hapter 2

Mike

Darkness is everywhere. The sound of crying babies echoes through the dark space. I hear women crying, begging for their lives. What's happening? Who could they be talking to? I could feel people touching; pulling on my pant legs. I swear it feels like they are talking to me. "How can I help you? Why are you asking me? I'm stuck here just like you!"

The voices and cries are so loud around me; then there is a "POP POP POP." I could hear people falling everywhere around me. Then the place got quiet and the only sound I hear was my own breathing. "Why don't they kill me too? Why am I the only one left standing? Lord please, just take me too. Don't leave me alone!"

Panic fills every fiber of my being; I feel the cold steel inside my hand. I smell the gun smoke in my face. Am I the killer? What kind of person am I? Don't they see that I'm afraid just like they were? How could they when I'm the one holding the gun.

My body is covered with sweat; pain shooting through my head like lighting. I start to shake; I could feel my body moving; I have no control over it. I could hear a light sound of beeping in the distance, and voices far away. Something is keeping me in this place; keeping me prisoner in my own mind. Slowly I could feel my body relaxing, but I am still in total darkness; darkness so cold, so scary. It is a coldness I could feel all the way down to my soul.

I try hard to open my eyes. I can hear the doctor calling me, but something is holding me here. I can hear the women and children again. I can hear them begging me for their lives. Then it all changed and this time I can hear a man's voice. It is different dealing with him. He isn't scared like the others. No, he is in control of everything. Then a picture forms in front of me. I can see him so clearly. It is like I was watching myself outside my body. I pull a gold 357 from the back of my pants and point it at him. He just stands there. He doesn't even try to move or run.

"You not gonna try and run dude? Go ahead. I will give you to the court of 5?" Then I hear myself start to court. "1 2 3 4 5."

"Do you really think I will give you the pleasure of running me down like a dog?"

"Well it would be more fun and make more sense, then you standing here looking like a fool,"

"Then you're wrong. If you're going to kill me, then do it right here and now with me looking you right in the eyes."

"Awww, what a noble death Steve, you ain't no fun. But what you fail to understand is the high of the kill still feels the same to me whether you run and hide or not."

"You are a cold hearted motherfucker. You know that Mike?"

"Yeah. I been told that a time or two." Then I pull the trigger.

My eyes open and I am face to face with my doctor who is standing by my bed.

"Are you alright? We have been trying to wake you now for the past 10 minutes."

"Yes, I'm alright. It was a bad dream I think. I can't really remember it."

"It's fine. Don't try to think on it too hard, we don't need another relapse. Things will come when they come. I called your family and they should be here soon."

"My family I haven't even begun to think about them, how could I face them like this? I don't know them anymore. I don't even remember who I am."

"Maybe when you see them things will begin to come back. We don't know just yet. Don't start getting yourself all worked up again. You just had a bad episode and the less stress you have the better."

Things are getting worse and worse. How would I begin to cope with this, when I can't remember anything in the first place? I know that dream meant something, but I don't remember what it's about. I have gotten to the point that I'm afraid to even go the sleep. This isn't the way for any fit man to live. It doesn't matter how much I try to fight sleep with all the medication they have me on, I feel like I have been drugged for days. Even in my drugged filled mind I know something isn't right with the way I've been living my life.

I close my eyes trying hard to picture someone from my family. Hoping to remember anything or anybody, but nothing is coming back to me. I hate living in this dark place. I feel so lost and so empty inside. It feels like more than my memory is missing. I can hear voices outside my door. I can tell that they are upset, but no one should be more upset then I am. I know I have heard that voice before, but for the life of me I can't put a face to it. A sharp pain shoots across my head then darkness took over.

Cory

I pace the hospital hallway back and forward. It kills me to know that my big bro has lost his memory. Maybe Jamaya is right. Maybe I should have taken over the business part of things while Mike has been here, but I'll never let her know that. One thing that I know is it isn't going to be easy, because Isaiah is the next in line for controlling our family.

Isaiah is the coldest of all of us. I don't have the heart to be dealing with him on that level. With Mike I can handle him, but Isaiah he is a different case all together. That is why I didn't want to push my luck in the first place. I kill for the business part of things, but Isaiah kills for the pleasure. You can see it in his eyes. I hate working with him, because he just gets too much joy out of killing people.

It's a rush for him, but for me it's only business and I let it be known with every hit. *"Money talk baby so this is only business."* It's my closing line with every mark. It's no sweat off my balls. I'm only stacking my papers. Don't nobody have a money hungry bitch like I do.

I opened the hospital room door slowly scared about what I am going to find looking up at me. Would he be the same person I've known all my life? Would he look at me and everything would come rushing back? God, I hope so and believe me I don't need this pressure right now.

He looks to be asleep which he is usually when I come to visit him. I look over at Jamaya and it killes me to know how much I need her strength right now. I reach for her hand and she takes it and holds on tight. I can feel the heat coming from her. Good, I need something to warm my body up again. I am so cold inside. It was like I have no feelings at all. I feel as lifeless as my bro lying in that bed.

She drops my hand and pulls me close as she wraps her arms around me. We just stand there holding each other. She lays her head on my chest and runs her small hands up and down my back. She never says one word. People always misjudge her and think that she doesn't have a heart, but I am able to look inside the heart of this scared woman and know I'm blessed with the love she has to give.

I don't know how long we stand there, but tears begin falling down my face.

Jamaya said in my ear, "Baby you know gangstas don't suppose to cry. So stop and let me do that for the both of us. "

Then she kisses me with so much passion and I know then that she loves me as much as I love her. She wipes my tears and traces the path with small kisses. "But it's understandable this time."

She doesn't know how much that meant to me to know that my baby doesn't look down on me, because I show a sign of weakness. Even if is only for a minute. Hell, even a gangsta killer cries sometimes.

Isaiah

I pull up to the hospital, music playing and smiling. I get to see my bro today and finally get some answers. No one knows how many people really lost their lives since Mike's has been here, but words out on the street that I've been on the war path so no one is talking. I have put my pistol to plenty people heads; so now they walk around the hood like they on pins and needles. No one knows when I'm going to hit next.

I feel my cell ring, but no one going to bring me down now. I am on a mission to finish what somebody else started. I can feel my blood pumping through my veins. This feels better then sex.

As I turned down the hallway near Mike's room I see a team of doctor's standing around with his chart in hand. As I get closer his doctor steps away from the group and walks toward me.

"My I speak with you for a moment Mr. Crawford?"

"Sure. Is something wrong with Mike?"

"You know that he was seriously hurt and with the gunshot wound to the head and all that swelling we came across a problem."

"Problem, what problem? Come on doctor just spit it out. What is going on with my brother?"

"He has lost his memory and we don't know if he will get it back in a day, month, or if ever."

"So you're telling me there isn't nothing you can do for him?"

"No it's not. He had another cat scan this morning and his brain still has a lot of swelling. He is having seizures back to back. Mike just might have to deal with them for the rest of his life."

"What about the wounds to his chest?"

"They are healing nicely. He hasn't gotten an infection in weeks. So the only thing we are worried about right now is the swelling around brain. Just be lucky that when he opened his eyes last night that he was even able to see. This is a good sign. Just give it a little more time and please don't try to push him to remember. It is only going to make things worse for him."

"Ok I want to say thanks for everything doctor." I watched as she turned and walked away. This was the first time that I wasn't turned on looking at her nice apple shape butt moving side to side as she walked away. I was frozen in place. I couldn't believe what I was just told. How the hell am I going to find out who tried to kill him?"

What if he never gets his memory back? This just can't be happening. All of my hopes just washed away. My smile dropped and I could almost feel my heart hit the floor. I turned heading back to the elevator when someone called my name.

"Isaiah."

I stopped but didn't turn around, because I knew just who was calling me.

"What you want Erica?"

"I came here to check on Mike since you can't seem to be around me anymore. What have I done for you to just walk away from me like that?"

"Look Erica I don't have time for this right now."

"Then tell me when are you going to have time because it don't seem like you are about to see your brother. From what I could tell you are heading in the wrong direction."

"What are you doing here? Are you stalking me? Believe me baby you don't want to go down that road with me?

"Stalking you!" She laughs. "Boy please don't get too high and mighty with that there, because you see how I look." She said as she turns around and gives him a view of her body. "I don't need to stalk no nigga."

"You know what Erica you're right you don't. Yeah you're fine as hell, but you hate it when someone doesn't pay you the time of day. Like me. Later shorty." I turned and hit the elevator button.

"You're a coward! I heard what the doctor said to you and now you don't even have the heart to face your brother, and to think I use to fuck around with you." She says as she pulls Mike's door open and walks inside.

I was left staring at the empty space that was still filled with the perfume I bought her. Damn bitch makes me sick. I hate it when she's right. Plus she knows how much that fly mouth of hers turns me on. We are like night and day. Don't have a thing in common, but when we get together we make fireworks.

I don't trust her so I have no choice but to follow her inside. When I open the door, not only was Erica in there but also Cory and Jamaya. It looks like I am the last one to get the news concerning him. Cory raises sad eyes to meet mine and I know he feels my grief.

The room is completely quiet and all that is heard was the beeping sounds from Mike's machines. I have all eyes on me even Mike's. It is like he felt that I came inside the room. He laid there not saying anything, but looking from face to face.

It is wonderful looking into my big bro eyes again, but you can tell that something is missing. Like a part of him is gone?

*C*hapter 3

Mike

My family is finally here and it is time for me to face them. I look at each person and can't remember a soul. I feel so out of place. I can see the sadness in their eyes and can almost feel their pain. It is all because of me. It's just too bad; I can't share in what they were feeling.

I want to say something, but I just don't know where to start. I am nervous and really want them to leave. I don't know these people, but we have to start somewhere,

"Well I take it that all of you know who I am? So could you start by telling me who each of you are?"

I looked at the guy closest to me and try to smile, but even a blind person can tell that it is forced.

"I'm Cory and I'm your youngest brother and this here." He pulled Jamaya closer to him and said, "This here is my girl Jamaya."

"And I am," The guy walked up to my bed. "I am Isaiah and that over there standing by the window is Erica,"

"That." I say with a smile. "Why do you call her that?"

"Forget you." Erica walks over to the side of my bed and places a soft kiss on my cheek. "How are you feeling today? As you can see not one of your brothers asked."

I laugh. "I'm better than I was yesterday I was told."

"I know that you want to know more about your life, but I think it would be better if we take our time," Isaiah say when he pulls out one of the chairs that is sitting in the corner.

"How will I ever remember anything if we sit here acting like everything is normal? I can't stand the fact I don't remember anything. You have to tell me something."

"Ok and what is it that you wanna know?" Cory said.

"Well, I see you have your ladies here, so tell me where is mine?"

"You don't have one." Cory and Isaiah say together.

"I don't have one? Not one lady friend."

"No you don't, and we've been behind you to change that for years, but you always say that they get in your way." Cory looks over at Isaiah hoping he hasn't said too much already.

"Get in the way of what? What is it that I am doing that I can't seem to settle down?"

Isaiah gets up, walks over the to the water jug and pours a cup of water. He hands it to me. I can tell he wants to say something, but he just freezes up.

"Look Mike we will get into that later."

"Oh I see how this going to be."

"And how is that?"

"Every time I ask you a question that you don't want to answer you just gonna push it aside like it doesn't really matter to me."

"No it's not like that Mike." Jamaya says. "The doctors said don't push it and we are not going to put too much on you today. Isn't it enough that you are learning all of us again? Please just take it one day at a time. I promise it will get better and things will start coming back to you."

"How about you try waking up and not remembering a damn thing and see how you feel."

Jamaya jumps up. "You see what I get for being nice to your ass. You still have that same fucked up attitude so you can rest a sure that ain't changed,"

"Well thank god something stayed the same. At least I have something to look forward to."

"And what is that?" she replies.

"At least I still can piss you off."

The look she gives me spoke volumes. I can tell she couldn't stand the ground I walk on. So I'm trying to figure out why the hell she's even here. There's more to her then met the eye.

"Little brother, you need to be careful. I'm telling you, something about that girl rubs me the wrong way."

Cory raises one eyebrow. "And what makes you say that?"

"It beats the hell out of me, it's just a feeling I'm getting."

"Are you sure you aren't remembering anything?" Cory prayed that he did because that sounded like the old Mike.

"Not a damn thing. Why you ask?"

"Never mind it doesn't matter anymore. So let me go and take her home. I will stop back by here later. Do you want anything back?"

"Naw I'm good." I watch as a smaller version on me walks out of the room.

Isaiah looks over at Mike and wonders if he doesn't really remember anything, because don't nobody talk that much shit in the predicament that he is in.

Cory

When I left Mike's hospital room Jamaya was madly pushing the down button on the elevator. Mike always had ways of getting under her skin, but I guess that went both ways. For a man who didn't know who he was his actions toward her were still the same.

It wasn't easy being in between the both of them, but the outcome would always be the same. When the elevator doors opened up I walked in behind her. Jamaya didn't say a word to me, but I know I'm going to get a piece of her mind when she does open her mouth.

I looked down at the top of her head. She was a small lady no more than 5'2, and the color of caramel. She had the most beautiful eyes I ever seen. They were hazel with little bits of green in them. Her lips were plump and kissable. Her body was what people call 24-36—

24. She was built right in all the right places.

"I can't believe you just sat there and let him talk to me like that." She yells not even looking at him.

"What you want me to do? The man is in the hospital for god's sake."

"I don't care what you would have done as long as you had done something. That's the thing with you; you always let him disrespect me. He feels like he can say anything to me."

"That's not true and you know it." I feel myself start to get loud.

"You always put Mike first and I hate that. Why do I have to come last to everything?"

"You don't come last to nothing, just drop it Jamaya. Damn girl you always find reasons to fight with me."

"Damn right, if you step up and be a man I wouldn't have to."

"What you say?"

"You heard me. I said if you step up and be a man then I wouldn't have to. What is it are you hard of hearing now?"

"You know what? I'm getting tired of this shit. You walk your little high and mighty ass around here like you got it like that. If it wouldn't for me you wouldn't have anything."

"And if it wasn't for me then… you know what never mind."

"Oh don't stop on my account what were you about to say?"

"You know me Cory I ain't the one to bite my tongue."

"Well, you sure as hell doing it now. Come on. You bad enough to say it go ahead say it dammit."

When the elevator comes to a stop Jamaya starts to walk out, but I pull her close to me. "I said say it!"

People were standing at the opening of the elevator ready to walk inside, but I could see the look of concern they had on their faces when they saw the way I grabbed her.

"What the hell you looking at? Y'all standing there like you ain't ever seen two people fussing before."

I don't loosen my grip at all. I pull her out of the elevator and continue walking out the hospital. In the background I can hear people saying, "Should we call security?"

"You have a way of making people feel sorry for you. They just don't know all the trouble that you cause."

"Let me go Cory! I mean it."

"Shut up and get in the car. You lucky I don't beat your ass right here. You're always somewhere showing out. I can't stand that shit. It's childish."

"I don't know who you talking to like that and I'm not childish."

"Jamaya this is my last time telling you get in the car or I'm going to leave you standing right there."

She jerks open the car door and gets inside slamming the door.

"Slam my door like that again bitch. I swear I'll knock the hell out ya."

She smacked her month. "You not gonna do nothing to me nigga that for damn sure."

She had her hair hanging loosely in a ponytail so I reach out and wrap it around my hand, slamming her face into the dashboard.

"And you better not get one drop of blood in my car either. Now clean yourself up."

I'm so tired of her sometimes I just want to leave her laid out on the side of the road.

Isaiah

I watch the way Mike interacted with us and something just isn't right. I could tell that he was missing bits and pieces of his memory. But no one sets out to upset someone, the way he upset Jamaya.

It don' t take a rocket scientist to know that he doesn't like her, but how does he know that if he doesn't remember anything. I really believe he's holding out on us.

"Erica could you give us a minute alone?"

"Why? You never had a problem talking in front of me before?"

"What's up with you anyway? Why are you even here?"

"Oh so now that you don't fuck with a bitch no more I'm supposed to just walk away from everything. Are you sure that's something you want me to do?"

"Walk away from what?" Mike asked. "What is she talking about?"

"She isn't talking about nothing Mike. Don't worry I'll handle this."

I grabbed Erica and pushed her out of the door shoving her all the way down the hallway toward the elevators.

"What the hell wrong with you girl? Are you losing your mind or something? You can't be seriously thinking about telling him about his past?"

"I can tell him anything I want. He ain't my brother."

"Listen and listen carefully Erica make this your last trip here, if I even catch wind of you being here again I will put you in a body bag. Is that clear?"

She looked me in my eyes standing almost 6 feet tall with her heals on. In all the time we been messing around I never said anything like that to her before. This was the first time that I ever saw her backs down.

"Oh so it's like that now?"

"Look baby this is my brother's health you playing around with. You know me, and if I say something I mean it no if ands or buts about it. You feel me."

"I know I'm sorry I was out of line. I will go and I won't visit anymore. I don't want to cause any problems."

"You won't cause problems if you just behave yourself like a lady should. I done told you about all that ghetto shit. I need a lady by my side not no damn hood rat. I know you came up in the projects baby but it's time to grow up and do what I say for a change. You the only person that gets away with that type of stuff you say."

"Well will I see you tonight, or you coming home?"

She walked up to me and wrapped her arms around my neck. She knew that drove me crazy when she rubbed her breasts up against me like that.

"I have to work tonight baby."

"Try that with someone else who don't know what you do."

"If it's done right it takes time. You can't be the best by rushing through things no matter how good the pussy is." I smiled and pulled her even closer for a kiss. That always seems to work and buy me a few more hours at least.

"Ok Mr. Professional just get your ass house by 1:00 am," Then she kissed me again.

I love the taste of her. I just can't get enough of her and she knows it too.

"One it is then. I will call you later baby."

Just like I said I know how to play her. I smile when she tapped her watch and said again "1:00 am". I swear that girl will be the death of me. I stood there long after the elevator doors closed trying to figure out how I could start testing my brother's memory. I took a deep breath, dropped my shoulders and headed back inside.

Veronica Meek

Chapter 4

Mike

I try hard to get what Erica said out of my mind but I can't. I'm just gonna have to ask Isaiah what she meant by that. It had to be important because of the way he rushed her out of the room. What are they hiding from me? It's driving me crazy not knowing the truth about myself.

I close my eyes trying hard to relieve the pressure I feel building up. Every time I turn around some damn nurse in here sticking on me. God I just wanna go home if I knew where that was.

Do I even still have a home? I know I must have lost my job being in here over 2 months. I'm not going to even think about how much this hospital bill is going to be. If I keep thinking like this I'm going to run my blood pressure up and I don't need another problem.

I rubbed my temple once again to ease my headache when flashes of memories start. I can see myself standing over someone. He is begging and praying for his life and saying "take the money". I can hear him so clearly. I heard this ugly laugh and I know that it came from me.

"I don't want your money fool. You know what I came from."

"Please man I'm begging you. I have a family and they need me."

"You should have thought of them before all of this."

"How could you say that? Please, man just don't kill me."

"Look you need to man up and take this here like a man shorty. This here is embarrassing. At least go out with some pride and not on your knees like some scared bitch. You made your bed and now it's time for daddy to lay you in it. How about this here; I will make it fast and quick. You won't feel a thing."

"God please forgive me for all my sins?" The man cried.

"God, I know you are not calling him now. It's too late, and there's nothing he can do for you. So go ahead and close your eyes and daddy will put you to sleep." I laughed.

He closed his eyes and continued to pray and as I pulled the trigger I heard him say, "God please forgive him he knows not what he do."

When I opened my eyes again Isaiah is standing there watching me.

"What did you just remember and don't say nothing because I know you would be lying."

"I just remembered killing somebody."

"Oh I see. Is that the first memory you have had like that?"

"It's the first memory, but I had a dream about me killing some women and kids, but it had to be just a dream right? I can't be going around killing people could I?"

"Please tell me you didn't tell anyone about this?"

"I'm not that crazy Isaiah I don't care how much of my memory is gone I wouldn't open my month and tell anyone I saw myself killing women and children."

"Good."

"Are you saying that it's true? I really did kill those people?"

"Mike listen to me I know this is a lot to take in right now, but give it time you will understand where all those memories are coming from."

"I don't want to give it time. I want to know if I am a killer Isaiah."

"Yes Mike. You are?"

"Oh... God!"

I drop my head in my hands and start to cry. How could I be so cold of a person to kill women and children? I just knew it had to be dream. I could never live with myself knowing that I did those kinds of things.

"I know it's hard to take in right now, but in time you will know why you are the way that you are."

"Leave, I need to be alone now."

"I don't want to leave you like this. I hope you're not going to say anything to anyone Mike. This is very important. Do you hear me?"

"I hear you, and believe me I'm not going to say nothing. I just need to be alone. I have to have time to take all this stuff in. Just leave I will see you tomorrow."

"Mike I can stay a little longer and help you figure things out if your memories are coming back now. You don't need to be going through this along."

"Tell me how could you make this earlier for me huh?"

"I don't know, but I can try."

"There isn't anything you can do. I have to learn to live with the fact that I was that type of person before."

"What you mean before? Mike that is who you are and it's who you will always be."

"I don't have to choose to live like that anymore and no one can force me to."

"You don't get it. What we do you just can't walk away from with or without memory lost."

"Are you telling me that this isn't by choice but this is what I do for a living?"

"Yes and there is no way in hell they are going to let you walk out. You got paid for what you love to do and you got paid well for it. There is no walking away Mike. Look all you are remembering is bit and pieces of things, but when it all comes back you will know your place."

"And where is my place?"

"You are head of our family. The one that makes all the decisions, and you're the one that took care of us when we had no one."

"I did all that?"

"You did all that and more my brother. Don't worry things will fall in place and you will once again know where you stand, but for right now I need you to continue to get better you feel me?"

"Yeah I got you lil bro."

I gave him a smile to reassure him that I am taking what he told me to heart. Which I am and soon I will know all I need to know about myself; the good, the bad, and the ugly.

Cory

After I hung up from talking to Isaiah I didn't want to believe what I just heard. How could someone be so weak now when he was so strong before? I can't believe he broke down and cried. I looked up to him for everything, and now I don't know this shell of a man that woke up in his place.

I'm glad I wasn't there when it happened. I don't know how I would have taken it, but deep down I believe I would have put a pillow over his face and let nature take its course. He wouldn't want to live being half a man, and I know that better than anybody. Isaiah always been closer to Mike then I have, but we loved him just the same.

He didn't have any favorites when it came to us. He would say we gangsta killers to the end, and dammit that's how we going to go out. All I know is that before I let the Mafia take him from us I will kill him my damn self.

Jamaya could see the change in me and knew that something was wrong. She tipped toed around me for hours since the incident in the car. She makes things harder than what they should be. I know I shouldn't hit her, but it's like she isn't happy until I'm treating her like trash.

I'm at my last straw with her. This was the first place I tried to set up roots. I even decided that it was time to have some kids. I am glad I waited as long as I did before trying, because that girl is unstable. I looked past some of the things she done in the past, but she went too far today.

I can hear her in the back on the phone. She been doing that a lot lately hiding out and looking over her shoulder making sure I'm not listening to her conversations. If she is fucking somebody I really don't give a damn. He can have her for all I care.

But something she said stopped me cold in my tracks so I stood there and listened.

"If you wouldn't have fucked up that nigga would be dead now." She stopped talking for a second I take it she was listening to the person on the other end. "What! I handed him right to you. So and he will never find out either. You just need to get your ass over to that hospital and put an end to him. That's all I have to say. I paid you damn good money. So finish him." She pushed the bedroom door shut and continued talking.

My blood ran cold. In my heart I knew she couldn't have been talking about no one other than Mike. I can't believe she tried to take my blood from me. All this time she looked me in my face while she had a knife deep in my back.

I wanted to walk away so bad. I didn't want to hear anymore, but I was glued to the spot. My blood was boiling to a point that I felt myself about to lose control; but I had to step back. I needed to find out just who she was working with.

If Isaiah ever gets wind of this he will kill her for sure and I can't let that happen. Oh, no she is all mine. When I'm finished with her she is gonna hate the day she ever set eyes on me and mine. The bedroom door opens up and she runs right into me.

"What the hell? Why you standing there looking crazy?"

I saw red as soon as she opened up her mouth. "Bitch it was you that tried to kill my brother?"

Once again for the second time that day I had my hands around her neck.

She tried hard to talk. "What are you talking about? I never did anything to Mike. Please let me go." She said thought uneven breaths.

"You're lying."

My hold around her neck tightens as I push her back inside the room and she landed hard on our bed. She is clawing and kicking so I stand over her and continue to choke her. I see the scared look in her eyes as the color drains from her face. I've seen that look a million times before, and she should know me enough to know that it doesn't faze me at all. What she doesn't know is that I have dreamed of this many times, and even came close a time or two.

But something stops me. Dying like this was too easy for her. I have other plans for her so I let go and stand up watching as she grabs her neck pulling hard and coughing. She starts to cry. When she had finally gets herself under control she reaches up to me.

"I'm sorry Cory. Please believe when I say that I didn't mean it."

"You sorry? Is that all you had to say? Like hell you didn't mean it. Why Jamaya?"

"I did it for you baby, for us. You have to believe me."

"Who did you send after my brother?"

"I can't tell you that baby, you know how these things work. Please let me try to fix it." She said as she tries to reach for her phone.

"If you touch that phone bitch I'll break your arm."

I reach over and pick up her cell and put it in my back pocket.

"Cory what are you doing? If you don't want your brother to die let me make that phone call."

I slapped her as hard as I could. "Don't you think you done enough?" I said as she went flying across the room. She hit the wall with so much force. Still I'm trying all I could not to kill her.

As I turned to walk away I pull out my cell and placed a call that I know will break my family apart. Isaiah listens without saying a word and when I am done the first thing he asks me, "Where is she?"

"Don't worry about her I have her under control. What you need to do is get back to the hospital."

"Do you think you can protect that bitch Cory?"

"If anything she needs protecting from me. Go I'm on my way."

When I turned around Jamaya is standing behind me. She has tears in her eyes and just for a moment I feel sorry for her, but only for a moment.

"He's gonna kill me isn't he?"

I just stood there watching the woman I love look like a scared little girl. She is shaken so badly, I hold out my arms and she runs into them. I held her like I wasn't going to hold her again. I smelled the shampoo in her hair as I did every time she's in my arms. I lifted up her head and wiped the tears from her face and kissed her.

I look deep in her eyes before I say. "Run!"

"What!" she drops her arms from around me? "What you mean run."

"You heard me." I yell. "Run and if I ever catch you, you're going to regret it."

I have nothing else to say to her. I hand her back her cell and head out the front door. Not once looking back.

Isaiah

I don't think I ever panicked before or even came face to face with fear but once in my life. I was only scared a few times before, and that was when I was a kid. Sometimes I could still hear our mother crying at night. I could see her taken beaten after beaten trying to protect us. Still to this day no one knew what was happening inside our home. No one ever heard us crying out.

Before our father died our mom was happy and one of the beautiful women in Madison. She had the longest hair I ever seen. It reached almost to the tip of her butt. Her skin color was tan almost like a caramel color, and she had light brown eyes which remind me of the color of hazelnut. Her cheek bones told a story about where she came from. You could tell she was mixed with something, but you just didn't know what. Her hair was long and red. She even had an Indian name (Lomasi) which means (Beautiful Blossom) but every one called her Lo Lo.

Our father was a proud black man and every one in Madison wandered how he ended up with a woman like Lo Lo, but it was love at first sight with them. Since the very first time he saw her he said that he was going to marry her; which he did. They were married almost 15 years before he died. He taught us everything he knew about hunting, shooting, camping, and even fishing. Hell we were real country boys.

It didn't take long for all of our innocence to be washed away. Mom married again and before long she realized that she made a terrible mistake. When she married George he didn't seem like he had a problem with her kids, but as time went by he found more and more reason to hit us and to send us to bed without supper. The beatings got so bad that one night George broke Cory's arm.

At first mom didn't mind she felt like we need a strong male around, but that was until the incident with Cory had gotten out of hand.

At that moment mom realized that she had to fight to help protect her boys, and we realized that we had to fight to protect her and ourselves, but we waited too late. We lost our mom soon after that. George stabbed her to death right in front of us.

I never had seen a look of hatred on Mike's face like I did that day. He fought until he couldn't fight anymore. He was so hurt and was barely about to walk, but he got Cory and me together and took us up to the attic to hide. Once we were up there Mike pulled out one of dad's rifles. As he loaded the gun I would never forget what he said, "Today boys we are going to become men, and we are going to make him pay for all he did. He will never hurt anyone of us again."

Mike pulled out the box of shells and handed it to me. I couldn't help but cry. I was so upset our mom laid downstairs dead and Mike was hurt badly. We were alone with a mad man in the house. We had to do whatever it took to protect ourselves.

It didn't take long for George to realize where we were hiding. We could hear his heavy boots coming up the steps.

"Hand me one of the bullets" Mike said.

My hand was shaken so bad that when I pulled one out the box it fell and hit the ground. I looked up at Mike and he put his hand on my shoulder to try to calm me down. Then he said. "It's ok Isaiah it will be over with soon. Go ahead hand me another one."

I reached inside and pulled out another bullet and placed it in his hands, but this time with little more confidence.

"Go ahead and get Cory and move over there."

We ran to the back of the attic and hide behind some boxes in the far corner. Mike walked over to the top of the stairs as he loaded the rifle; the sound echo through the whole room. I could hear the footsteps stop so I knew he was at the top of the stairs. I pulled Cory in my arms and held him close. I looked over the top of the boxes I could see George standing in front of Mike, and you could still see our mother's blood dripping from the knife George held in his hand.

When Mike shot the rifle I nearly jumped out of my skin. I just couldn't believe he done it. I heard George say, "You really had the nerve to shot me you little fuck." George punched Mike in the stomach and he dropped the gun and fell to his knees. George kicked the rifle away from Mike and start pounding on him.

I looked down at Cory and I could tell he was scared, but I had to help Mike. "Cory stay right here I have to go help him."

* * *

I crawled over to where the first shell had landed and slowly pulled one of the rifles over to me. I tried so hard not to make a sound, but as I open the rifle and slide the bullet inside and the rifle clinked. George turned his head and looked toward me. Then he smile.

"What you gonna do with that boy. You ain't got the balls your brother got." George said as he begins to turn his back to Mike.

"You're wrong."

I aimed the rifle and shot. Once the sound and the smoke cleared George was still standing there. I was scared that I missed him, as I ran and grabbed the box of shells he fell to the ground. I stood there and watched as George took his last breath. After that day we never were the same.

That day played back in my mind all the way back to the hospital. Somehow it feels like the same as before, but this time slightly different. My brother lying there not able to protect himself with someone standing over him trying to kill him. How history repeats itself.

I hope I make it there in time. We just had a scare for his life and sometimes it feels like it's never going to be over. I knew I shouldn't have left him in the first place. Something deep inside told me to stay. Why didn't I listen to it? I swear if anything else happened to my brother because of Jamaya; killing would be too good for her, but either way she's a dead woman.

A DEAD WOMAN...

Chapter 5

Mike

Sleep was a long time coming. I didn't know how to react to what I just learned about myself. How could I be that person when inside I feel as innocent as a new born baby? No matter how much I try memories continued to come back, but that empty feeling I had since my mother was killed wasn't there anymore. All I had was just a lot of emotions that I don't know how to control.

Tears started to fall once again and it killed me to see how weak I had become. I understood where Isaiah was coming from. I know I can't just walk away, but I don't want to live this life anymore. I can't be responsible for taking any more lives. How many sons have I taken from their mothers? How many fathers' have I taken from their kids? How many husbands have I taken from their wives? I am a monster and a cold blooded killer. Everybody in the hood referred to us as the "Gangsta Killer's".

I closed my eyes and prayed for all the people who lives I have taken away from them. I prayed to be forgiven for all of my sins. Would he ever forgive me? Only time would tell. I heard my room door open but I just didn't have the heart to open my eyes and face the world. For all I knew I could have taken one of their love ones away from them. It could have been one of their sons, brothers, or fathers'. It's just best I lay here and pretend I'm sleep. It would be best for everyone if I just wasted away.

Then suddenly I felt something land across my face. I tried to open my eyes and even tried to scream. I tried to fight, but I had no strength at all. It was so hard to breath and my mind was calling out for help. "Oh god someone is trying to kill me!" I could feel the hand that was pressing down on my face. My chest felt like it was about to explode. All the air was gone as my lungs start to burn.

It was funny how I was just wishing I was better off dead and now I'm here fighting for my life. My hands flew up and I knew I was touching the face of my killer. I tried to wrap my arms around their neck, but I just couldn't get a good grip. I felt my body getting weaker and weaker. My heart was nearly beating out of my chest. As I felt my arms drop down and my breathing slowed I knew that my time was running out and I was dying that night.

I didn't have any more fight left in me. I felt so beaten and for the second time in my life I'm in a situation that I wasn't able to control. I was powerless to help myself just like I was all those years again with my mother. Just thinking about her I could see her so clearly. She smiled at me and reached her arms out for me. I could feel her embrace as her arms wrapped around me. She was still as beautiful as the day she was taken from us.

She pulled back and smiled once again. "My son you have to go back."

"But why can't I stay with you? What if I don't want to go back?"

"Baby it isn't your time just yet." She ran her hand down the side of my face. "Your brother's need you."

"You don't understand mom I just can't. You just don't know all I have done."

"I know everything that you have done, and believe me baby you are forgiven. God understand the path that you and your brother's took. So stop worrying about him judging you. We are all put here to live out our lives. Please baby fight for me. Please go back. Open your eyes baby."

"How could you plead for me to go back when I am as cold blooded a killer as George? How am I different?"

"Mike listen to me you can't stay here. Go back now."

"No mom I can't leave you again. I want. I miss you and I love you so much."

"And I love you too baby that's why I'm telling you to go back. Go back now you're running out of time. Please Mike please go back I'm begging you!"

I could hear the emotion in her voice and saw the tears in her eyes. I hate to let her down. Even though I wanted nothing more than to stay here with her and leave this life behind. It would have hurt my mother worse with me staying here and not going back to help protect my brothers. She was so sure that they needed me. I had no choice, but to let go of the warm embrace my mother place around me and ease back into that cold dead body I left behind.

Cory

I drove to the hospital like I 'm driving in the Atlanta Motor Speedway. My tires burned the highway like I was trying to win the World Cup. Never had I been so afraid in my life. How could I be so blind when it came to my brothers? I never had been so stupid about love before. Never this blind that I couldn't see through any of her shit. Jamaya really had my heart messed up and I have no one to blame but myself. If anything else happened to my brother I don't know if I would ever forgive myself.

I pulled into the hospital parking deck and slam to a stop. When I hopped out I spotted Isaiah running down the parking lot heading for the lobby. I wasn't even sure I closed my car door before I was out and headed in the same direction.

It took the elevators forever to arrive so I headed for the stairs. I'm not in shape like I use to be. I think to myself taking two steps at a time all the way up the five flights. Just as the elevator doors opened up I blast out the stairwell door. Isaiah didn't even stop, but ran past me and on down the hall towards Mike's room. When I got inside the room I came face to face with Isaiah holding a man from behind pulling him off of Mike.

I opened the room door back and looked out making sure that the hallway was still clear. Inside of my jacket pocket I pulled out a long piece of wire and came up behind Isaiah and wrapped it around the guy neck. Isaiah pulled something out of Mike's draw and stuffed it inside the guy's mouth. I wrapped the wire around his neck even tighter and pulled until he started sliding down to the floor. I didn't stop choking him until his eyes were damn near popped out of his head. When I finally let go and let the body fall to the ground Isaiah had already pulled the pillow off of Mike's face.

"Is he dead? Are we too late?" I asked sounding winded.

"He's barely breathing, but we made it. Quick push that nigga under the bed so we can call and gets him some help."

I didn't even bend down to push him under. I used my foot and kicked him under the bed. Once that was done Isaiah pushed the button and the red light started blinking. To me it seem like it took forever for that scene to play out, but to be honest all that happened within a couple minutes. I don't believe I ever took someone out that fast before. I wish I could have taken my time. I would have loved to see and hear the fear coming from him, but it's all good, because soon Jamaya would take his place.

The nurses came in and the first thing they notice was the way Mike looked. So one of them rushed over and pushed the button for CODE RED. We both knew what that meant and we could tell just by looking at him that Mike was in serious trouble. Once his doctor arrived in the room and did an exam on Mike the first question out of her mouth was, " What happened to him?"

"I don't know doctor we just arrived here." Isaiah tried to explain.

The doctor leaned over Mike and opened each of his eyes looking into them with a flash light. "His eyes are out of focus and his heart rate is through the roof. What did you do to him?"

"Wait a minute now just what the hell are you saying?" I walked over to where she was standing. "Are you trying to say that we did something to hurt our brother?"

"What I am saying is that something happened here and I want to know right now before I call the police."

"I can't believe this shit. We been waiting for months for our brother to wake up and you are accusing us of trying to hurt him."

"They didn't do anything to me." Mike said but his voice was low and weak. "I could not lay here and listen to this any longer. As you can see I'm ok but I would like for you to give me something for the pain."

"I can't give you anything as long as your heart rate is speeding like this. I hope you aren't protecting them Mike, because if they tried to hurt you we could help you, and move you where no one could reach you."

"Didn't he say that we didn't do jack shit to him lady? Why are you not listening?"

"I am listening, but I can also see that something happened here. Mike is my only concern not whatever you say."

"Are you finished looking over my brother, because if you are we could use some privacy."

I like her nerve. For all these weeks Isaiah and I have been nothing but supporting when it came to our brother.

How could she even think we would hurt him?

"I have to run some more tests on him to make sure nothing seriously happened after this attack."

"Attack and what on earth makes you think that he was attacked?" Isaiah said trying hard to push the doctor from that frame of thinking.

"Yes if he had another seizure then I have to see if the swelling has returned."

"Oh that kind of attack."

"Yes and what kind of attack did you think I was speaking of?"

"I didn't know. That's why I asked."

"Listen guys if I find out that you're in here pushing him to remember then I am going to have to stop visitations until he is better."

"Yes we understand." I smile. "You got us it will not happen again."

"I hope not. Will you excuse me?" The doctor picked up Mike's hospital chart and exited the room with the staff following close behind.

I watched as they exited then looked over at Mike. He still looked a little shaken but that was understandable after what he just went through.

"Now would you two mind telling me why the hell this pussy nigga just tried to kill me?"

I looked over at Isaiah hoping he would take over, but he gave me the evil eye. "Don't you think you need to start talking?"

"But.."

"But nothing and you know it would be much better coming from you."

"What the hell you two talking about? All I know is somebody better tell me what the fuck is going on." Mike was angry and for the first time they both could see that they wasn't dealing with that same confused person they left behind hours ago.

I closed my eyes and decided to start at the beginning. I told him about the fight Jamaya and I had when we left out of his room this morning. How she said things that had me thinking, and how I made my mind up to leave her. And finally how I walked down toward our bedroom and I overheard her on the telephone.

Mike didn't say a word. Not even an "I told you so", but as I continued to talk I knew he was getting madder and madder. Then his voice ricocheted through the room, "You did what?"

"You heard what he said Mike." You could see the vein popping out the side of Isaiah forehead.

"I said I let her go." I said as I looked Mike in the eyes. Today wasn't the day to show him any fear.

Isaiah

I stood back and watched as my two brothers went head to head. It was just like old times; it almost had me smiling. Almost. It pained my heart to see Cory in so much pain and having to choose between the woman he loves and his brother. I know it had to be hard on him. Yeah he said he was about to leave her, but it isn't the same. Just because you walked away doesn't mean you would stay away. Now he has to hunt her down and it's not for good. That is if I don't find her first.

I had always been a gangsta killer. I haven't killed anyone other than that. No women, no kids; just gangstas. That's how we got our name, but now people are putting hits out on any and everybody. It just doesn't matter anymore. When it came to taking out whole families I left that to Mike. Just because I'm cold didn't mean my heart was black.

I looked under the bed wandering how we going to get old dude out of here. Killing him was the easy part, but removing this fool was the problem. I didn't want to interrupt them, but this situation needed to be handled before someone spotted him.

"Have anyone of you thought of a way to get him out of here?"

"My mind is on other things right now." Mike said through tight lips.

"Other things like what?"

"Believe me you don't want to know."

"What Mike? You ain't said enough all ready?" Cory said angrily,

"You lucky I can't get up out of this bed."

"And if you could what you gonna do huh?"

"I would beat your ass for starters. I told you to leave that bitch alone a long time ago, but did you listen. Hell no."

"You have some balls talking shit to me when you weren't even strong enough to take that pillow off your face a moment ago."

"What you say?"

"You heard me. Why you need me to say it again?"

"Ok now that's enough! We don't have time to be fighting. What we need to do is try to figure out how we gone get this dude out this hospital, the sooner the better." I said.

"Hell why don't you two just walk him out for god sakes. Believe me ain't no one going to notice this in a hospital. All they going to think is that he is sick of something.

"What! You think it's easy to just walk a dead body out of the hospital?"

"Yes." Mike said.

"You must be crazy! You tell me how in the world we going to pull that off?"

"I believe it will work Isaiah. I really do." Cory agreed.

"Well we might as well get started then. Go look and see if the nurses' station still empty." I told Cory.

"I didn't believe you even noticed that the way you flew past there." Cory said on his way to the door. He opened it up and looked outside. "Give me a second I'm going to walk the halls for a minute."

While Cory was gone that give me a minute to talk to Mike about the way he was dealing with things concerning Cory. The last thing we need is for Cory to find her first and help her escape.

"Mike we need to talk."

"That's all we seem to do now is talk. What's on your mind brother?"

"I think you need to be careful with the way you dealing with Cory. That's all we need is for him to be protecting her."

"Do you really think that would be something that he would do?"

"No I don't, but you will never know. You of all people know how much he loved Jamaya. I mean why else would he have not killed her while he had the chance."

"You're right. I just can't help but be upset, you know."

"I know, but it isn't really his fault. It wasn't like it was something that he planned."

"But how could we really know?"

"I can't believe you just said that Mike. You know he would never do anything to hurt either one of us."

"I know, but sometimes I can't help but think it. You feel me."

"I ain't going to lie it crossed my mind too, but I trust him. I'm not gonna let some stupid ass bitch take that away from me."

There wasn't anything left to be said on the subject; it was a good thing because Cory chosen that moment to walk back inside the room. He didn't even look at us.

"It's clear. Go on pull dude out from under there, so we can get this over with." Cory said.

When I removed him from under Mike's bed, the guy had already starting to stiffen up. Cory walked over and helped me pull him up right and toss an arm around my neck and his. We had almost made it to the door, when that damn doctor walked right back in. We froze in place.

Nothing came to mind to explain the situation at the moment. Someone had to think and fast. I was wondering who it was going to be.

"Just what is going on here? Is he alright?"

"Oh yeah he's fine. Why you asking?" I replied.

"Let me check him and make sure. Put him down over there in that chair."

"No he's good. There's no need for you to concern yourself, doctor."

Are you sure you don't need me to check him out? It won't be a problem."

"No he's good, just got a little too excited when he realized that Mike gotten his memory back that's all." Cory lied with a smile.

"Ok if you're sure."

"Believe me we are. Mike we'll check on you later man, and doctor make sure he gets some rest."

I didn't even hear their replies. We left the room with as much speed as we could muster while lugging dead weight.

Veronica Meek

Chapter 6

Mike

I watched as they walked the body out of the room, but I could clearly see that the doctor had something on her mind. I hoped she couldn't tell they were carrying a dead man.

"So doctor what brings you back so soon?"

This is one sexy woman. What I wouldn't do to get my hands on her.

"I was worried about you and wanted to see for myself that you were okay before I left for the night."

"As you can see I'm doing well. Thank you for caring about me. Tell me are you this concerned about all of your patients?"

"No not all of them. Why do you ask?"

"I just wanted to know."

"Mike you've been here for a while now. It seemed like I had been waiting for you to wake up for years." She dropped her head like she was kind of unsure about what she was saying.

"What's your name? I like to call you something else other than doctor sometimes. Please have a seat. Stay and talk to me for a while." I pointed to the seat closest to my bed.

She gave me a smile and reached out and grabbed my hand, then she sat down on the edge of my bed.

"My name is Makalya Daniels." She said while pointing to her name tag. She held onto my hand a little longer and then placed it softly on her leg.

I looked at her because I couldn't believe that she was making things very clear about how she was feeling. So I decided to see how far she would let me go. I begin to run my hand up and down her leg. Then inch by inch I slide it under her doctor's jacket. Her skin was so soft, smooth, and warm; it felt like I hadn't touch a woman in a much longer time than a few months. I pulled my hand away from her and dropped it beside me.

"I shouldn't have done that?"

"It's what I wanted."

"Well it shouldn't be. You need to stay away from me." I said and turned my back to her.

"Don't turn your back on me Mike." She pulled me back around to face her. "Tell me why I should stay away from you?"

"Because I'm no good for you that's why."

"How could you say that?"

She got upset. She couldn't believe I wouldn't even give her a chance.

"You don't know me and you wouldn't know what you would be getting yourself into."

"I want to get to know you, and I don't care. I want to be with you Mike. What is it? Am I'm not pretty enough for you."

"What! Girl, you are one of the most beautiful and sexy woman I have ever seen."

"Then why don't you want me?"

"Makalya I never said that I didn't want you. I said I'm no good for you. Come here baby."

She leaned down and when my lips touched hers I just knew that we were meant to be together. She could warm this cold and empty heart of mine. Now I was beginning to understand why my mother sent me back.

She felt so good in my arms and still I wonder do I deserve someone like her in my life. How could I make someone like her happy? She is used to living one way and I'm used to another. How would this even work out? I have to pull away from her. I don't deserve her or anybody for that matter. The type of life I live is meant to be lonely.

I looked deep in her eyes, and I could see that she meant everything that she said. She really had developed feelings for me. Would it be wrong to enjoy her company just until I got out of here? Then I walk away and never look back. I promised that I would never let her suffer because of me.

I know that when I walk out of her life, so would the devil himself. She wouldn't know what kind of life she was in store for messing around with someone like me.

She laid her head on my chest. I could feel the pressure and pain from it, but it didn't matter. I wouldn't let some gun shots wounds to the chest take away something that I had been missing for so many years. So I pulled her closer and enjoyed the feel of her.

She heard my sharp intake of breath.

"Oh, am I hurting you? Let me up."

"No, stay there just let me hold you a little while longer." She smiled and kissed me softly.

"It's ok baby it's only a little pain. It's making me stronger."

I laid back and enjoyed the feeling of my woman no matter how long she would be in my arms. I closed my eyes once again not afraid to fall asleep since the first moments I opened my eyes.

"All In The Name Of Love"

I have a knife deep in my back

And a thirst for blood

All in the name of love

I have tears in my eyes

Trying hard to push these feeling aside

This made one of the strongest of men cry

All in the name of love.

I have hate in my heart

Hurt and fear going thru my veins

All in the name of love.

You have me running around about to go insane

I couldn't believe all the drama you bring

All in the name of love.

You said you done it for me but it was really for you

You knew all along what you were going to do

Now you have me here wondering what we had was true.

All in the name of love.

Cory

I felt like Tupac "All Eyes On Me" as we walked dude out of the hospital. I still can't believe that it really worked. We were nearly dragging him when we arrived at the parking deck. He gave another name to the phrase dead weight.

"Where is your car at Cory?" Isaiah asked me.

"I can't believe you asking me that. You're the one with the truck. I'll catch hell trying to get him inside my car."

"This is your mess so you going to finish it." Isaiah looked at me and I knew he wasn't going to let it go. I inhaled and pointed toward the right.

"It ain't no need for all that breath blowing because you know it's only fair. So take my truck and I'll get it from you later."

I could feel my phone vibrating on my hip it's been going off since I left the house. My mind went back to my last time seeing Jamaya. I could see the sad look on her face. I could still hear her crying as I was walking out the door.

I been moving on fumes since this shit happened. It feels like I lost everything in one day; my girl and my brothers. Right now I'm moving like a machine. I'm just doing it. I didn't snap out of it until I hear Isaiah's truck door close with the dead man inside.

I couldn't even think clear. My mind is like jelly. How could things be this messed up? I heard my brothers talking about me. How could they even doubt me? I have proven myself over and over again. How could they believe some woman could come between us? It was the hardest thing to do to stand there and listen and not defend myself.

Yes I love her and I know it's going to be hard to walk away and not look back. There isn't a woman in the world I could see myself with other then her. Maybe they are right. Maybe I should take her and run, but they would never stop looking for her. If I choose to leave; they would never stop looking for me either.

I pulled my cell out and read my texts.

"I know your mad with me but ain't no one gonna love you like I do."

How could she even think that? If she really loved me she would have never done anything like that.

Then I read another one. "I told you I'll be with you no matter what. How could you just walk away and leave me?"

Still I didn't reply. Why is she trying to hold on to something that might take her life? Why isn't she leaving and trying to protect herself? I just don't understand how someone so smart could be so stupid.

Once again my cell went off. I didn't even bother to look at it. I started the truck and rolled out of the parking space. It wouldn't take long to get rid of ole boy. I know just the place for him.

It was killing me to know what she really had to say. So when my phone rang again I answered it.

"Yeah." I didn't hear anything just sniffing. "What do you want Jamaya?"

"I want you to talk to me."

"I am talking to you. Now what do you want?"

"I want you to forgive me."

"You know I can't do that?"

"Please baby. I can't live without you."

"Don't worry you won't?"

"What that supposed to mean?" She starts to cry.

"Now baby you already know. I just don't understand why you doing this to yourself?"

"I love you Cory and if losing my life is what it would take to make things right with us then I would happily do it."

I didn't want to hear that. God she is making this so hard for me and she knows that.

"Where are you?"

"Why are you coming for me?"

"Don't be silly girl. Where are you? Please don't tell me you still at home."

"No, I'm not there. I'm not crazy you know. If I stayed there I would probably be dead by now."

"How do you know that?"

"Because Isaiah couldn't be with you, and if he were you wouldn't be talking to me right now."

"Where are you?" I asked again.

"If I tell you would you come and get me so we can leave?"

"Do you really think leaving is going to solve our problem?"

"All I know is that I just want to be with you. Can I at least spend one more night with you? Then I will leave I promise, and you will never see me again."

I pulled the truck over on the side of the road. I couldn't drive because my hands were shaking too much. If she's tells me where she at, I don't know if I would be the one to take her life or save it right now.

Isaiah

I watched the back taillights of my truck as it flew down the expressway. I could clearly see that Cory was still in contact with Jamaya. It was only a matter of time before he would lead me right to her. As I passed my truck sitting on the side of the road I saw that he having a heated conversation.

My mind went back to the conversation Mike and I had, believe I was wishing I was wrong about him. I pulled over at the next exit. I knew where he was taking the body this locations was one of our favorite spots. I didn't have to sit long before he flew pass me.

I was tempted to go by his house but something told me that she wouldn't be there. She might be crazy but she was far from stupid. One thing I noticed about her was that she always had a hold over him. I didn't see a need to worry about that, because it never affected his work. Mike wanted to take her out a long time ago once he seen the impact she had over his life.

I thought about my relationship with Erica and I knew I didn't have room to talk, but Erica is controllable even if she has me wrapped tighter than a rubber band. That's one thing I know for sure, she would never do anything like that. It wasn't about power with her it was all about money. The only power she liked was the power I had over her. That was a turn on for her.

It has been one hell of a day and it wasn't anything I would like better than being knee deep inside my baby's body. What I needed right now was a release. I decided to drive close the where Cory would be and turned the car in the other direction. I pulled over to the side and let the darkness cover up the car.

I know he would be down there for a while, so I pulled out my cell and called my baby. I already know I am going to have to hear her mouth because I might not make it in.

"Hey baby what you doing?"

"I'm waiting on you. Why. Where you at?"

"I told you that I might not come home tonight."

"I think you over some hoe's house."

"Think Erica. If I was over some hoe's house, would I be on the phone with you?"

"Knowing you? Yes."

I laughed. "No baby I'm working. What you got on?" I reached down and touched my manhood.

"I'm not telling you. I know what you about to do."

"What; I'm not about to do anything."

"Yes you are, and you're not going to get your rocks off and leave me over here wanting."

"Erica have I ever left you wanting baby?"

"No." She moaned. "I don't know. You had been acting so funny lately like you don't want me anymore." She moaned again this time a little louder.

"I would always want you. Are you touching my special jewel for me baby?" I unzipped my pants and pulled my rock hard manhood out of the hole in my boxers.

She made another soft moan in my ear. "Yes I am."

"Is it wet for daddy?"

"So wet baby and mommy ready for you to come and taste it. You wanna taste it daddy?"

I licked my lips and I could almost taste my baby. "Damn baby I could almost taste you. I wanna smell that pussy,"

"You know I love it when you talk like that."

"And I love it when you give me what I want anyway I want it."

"You can have it any way you want too baby just come home and get it."

She continued making those soft little sounds that I love as I rub myself. My man was jumping in my hand. There wasn't anything else to say. There were noises coming from both ends of the phone. I could hear her breathing starting to move faster. Then I started moving faster, and faster.

"You about to cum for me baby."

"Yes Yes Yes!" I could hear her explode and I let one out right behind her.

"Hmmmm." I said. "Now that was good baby. Now go get in the shower and get all oiled up for daddy and I'll be home soon."

I didn't even wait for her to reply I hang up the phone and looked around for something to clean myself up with. I know he had to have something in here.

As soon as I cleaned up I saw the first signs of headlights in the mirror telling me that Cory was coming back up the wooded path. I opened up the front door and pulled my lighter out of my pocket then lit the napkin on fire that I found on the floor in the back of car.

There is no way in the world I would be leaving any evidence around here. I watched as the napkin quickly burned and left nothing but aches. I closed the door and turned the car on and pulled out right behind him. I hate to disappoint Erica but I wouldn't be coming home anytime soon tonight.

.

Chapter 7

Mike

The night didn't seem as bad as Makayla lays in my arms, but it wasn't long before she had to go. My mind continues to go back and forward on my brother's; wondering what was going on with them. It wasn't so bad not knowing what they were doing, but it was worst not knowing if I could trust one of them.

I know I can't solve all of our problems over night so I might as well get some sleep. It just surprises me that the police haven't showed their faces here yet. It don't matter if they come or not since ain't nothing they can do this is family business. What happens in the family stays in the family.

Just speak of the devil; the police walk in with pads in hand. I already knew that they were told that I lost my memory, but still they're here just like clockwork.

"Mr. Crawford I was told you came out of your coma. Sorry it took so long to stop by it's been a busy day." The officer looked at his watch like he was checking the time. "My name is Detective Williams and this here is Detective Wilkins." He held out his hand for me to shake.

"Nice to meet you officers, so what can I do to for you?"

"We would like to see how much you remember about the day that you were attacked."

"I'm sorry but I don't remember anything at all about that day."

"You mean that you don't remember who shot you?" Detective Wilkins asked while writing in his pad.

"No I don't remember anything at all. I wish I could help you but right now I can't. So if you don't mind can you turn the lights off on your way out? I would like that a lot. Thanks for stopping by."

"Mr. Crawford I know that you been through a lot but it would really help if you could tell us something about what happened that day."

"As I just said Detective Wilkins if I could remember something I would tell you, but since I don't. There isn't anything left for me to say. I don't see any reason for me to be wasting your time or you mine. Now if you would excuse me I would like to get some sleep I have had a very long day."

"Here is my card if you remember anything please give me a call."

I took the card and placed it on the table beside my bed.

"Thank you I will do that and have a nice night fellas."

I saw that they could see that I was marking them. This was family business I don't need them all up in it.

I have other things to be dealing with. Soon some of my clients are going to be making their selves know, trying to see if I'm able to be trusted or not. As soon as I get one person off my back here comes a hundred more.

I closed my eyes trying to ease my mind so I could sleep, but it was just too much going on around me that my nerves were going haywire. Why would Jamaya fuck things up like this? I hope they find her soon; for all that I know she could be off hiring someone else to finish me off.

People always say keep your friends close and your enemies closer, but not anyone said a damn thing about family. What would they do when it all fell into their laps? Would they kill her, or would one brother protect the other one and hide the bitch. I wish I could get out of here and take care of it myself. God, I feel so useless, and laying here like this isn't helping. The way I feel right now I can't trust anyone but myself.

I pulled the covers up over my shoulders and try hard to block out all the demons that's surrounding me. Wishing I could once again be wrapped in my mother's warm embrace. For the first time I understood what they meant when they said "Peace in heaven and hell on earth". Every since I opened my eyes this morning I have been in hell.

Things just have to get better from this day forward. My family has to get our unbreakable bond back. We have been through too much to fall apart now. I lay here watching my memories play out in front of me like a movie. The more they returned the more I felt like my old self.

All the memories did was made me wish that I could have stayed that innocent, but it wouldn't have lasted long. The people around me wouldn't have let it. I was put on this earth to kill.

When my judgment day comes I already know I'm going to burn in hell. So I have prepared myself for that day, but until then I will enjoy and live every day to the fullest.

Jamaya

As I lay across the bed in my hotel room everything that I have done flashes a cross my mind. I never believed that things would have gotten this out of hand. I pressed redial again and listened as Cory's phone went to voice mail. I don't have anywhere to go. I could never go back to my family. The only person I had was Cory and I found a way to mess that up just like I have done everything else in my life.

He doesn't know all the things that he should about me, I tried hard to keep it that way. Cory would never understand the person that I am or where I came from. I have to prove to him that I'm worth keeping. I know his heart is cold toward me right now. If he just answers the phone maybe I could get him to forgive me. I know he would. All he has to do is give me a little of his time, so I can prove to him what I did was necessary.

If he doesn't listen to reason I still have one trump card to use. I know it would work. He could never hurt me or our baby then. I haven't told him about my pregnancy. If he knew about the baby he would be on my side and I wouldn't be here alone, scared and afraid for my life.

I close my eyes and remembered the reason I set all of this in motion. Cory was home that day mad about Isaiah getting more work than he was. Mike always favored Isaiah over him and that always pissed him off. It got to the point when it did the same to me. I know how the game works I been around it all my life. So I know when someone is being fucked over. I hated that Cory felt that he was the outcast of their family. He complained about it often. All it did was set the wheels turning on a plan to set Mike up.

It didn't matter what I did to try to make things comfortable for Cory at home all I did was make him mad with me even more. I could hear my father clearly; *"Maya no matter what you say or do you always find a way to get yourself caught up in shit."* He was right so I'm not going to lie. I did things a lot to make him go off. But sometimes it was just the stress of the job. People just don't know but its hard being a Gangsta Wifey. Yes I wanted nice things. I wanted to drive nice cars, live in nice houses, and wear nice clothing, but I didn't think of all the pressure it put on him to get those things for me. Hell I grew up with all that and I didn't see my father bring home his problems.

Cory came in my life at a time in my life that he ended up being my savior. I couldn't help but cry. I cried for all the wrong I have done to the man that I love. I cried because now he has to choose between us or them. Who would he choose; His family or ours. Would he be able to look at me and know that I wouldn't ever do anything to hurt him? My mind went back to the day I decided to solve our problems with Mike.

I was shopping at Lenox when I overheard some guys walking and talking about Mike. Just hearing his name caught my attention so I followed then into a restaurant and picked the table right behind them and I listened. They talked about all the things Mike had done to them. How he robbed the low level dealers as well as the kingpins that where supplying them. How he was making it hard for anyone to come up. They were getting tired of it.

So yeah hearing that shocked me. I knew Cory didn't know anything about that piece of side money Mike was making. The guys continued talking not even caring how their voices carried around the restaurant or who were listening to them.

So I had my ears glue to their table listening to their every word. Mike was a mobster not only a killer, but he robbed anyone he pleased and no one did a thing about it. Just because of who he was. They were wondering how long he would keep robbing the people that he weren't working for, because it was only a matter of time before he would start blasting the heads of everyone no matter who they were.

I was so busy thinking of a plan and how to use that information that I was eye balling their table. I was listening so hard that I didn't even notice that they stopped talking and were looking right at me. So I smile and being who I am I got up and introduced myself. I could tell that they were taken aback because they knew just who I was, but they listened and was glad to see that it was a way they had an inside link and could finally take down the mighty Mike Crawford.

When I started my day it wasn't something that I had planned to do; I didn't just set out to have Mike killed. I listened as they talked and informed me of what they expected of me. What they asked for wasn't hard at all. All they wanted me to do was get Mike to a place where they could catch him alone.

You see growing up in Florida with a family like mine, things had to be done right so I decided to pay them. I didn't want a half ass job done and still those fools botched the job. How could someone survive 5 fatal gunshot wounds? For months no one knew what really happened to Mike and they wouldn't have if I haven't been trying to get them to clean up their mess.

Now once again I'm the reason why things are messed up like this. I'm the reason why I have lost my family. I'm the reason why I lost the man I love, and I'm the reason I'm about to lose my life along with my child. I knew in my heart that

Cory would never forgive me he was so much like my father. That's why I was so drawn to him. As I rode around today I was still wondering why he let me live. Why did he stop? He had me right where he wanted me? Maybe our love could out do all the wrong I have done, but if my own family couldn't forgive me for what I did how could Cory.

I laid in the dark and cried. I let all the pain flow through me because I will never know what tomorrow could bring. I opened up my cell once again and the light shined through the room. I hit redial and listen to Cory's voice on his voice mail once again.

Cory

I watched as the headlights shines in my rearview mirror and smiled. All that time Isaiah had been following me. I don't know if he thought I'm crazy or what but doesn't he know that I know my own car. So I take it what I overheard was their true feeling. They don't trust me but that's too bad. They are the ones who have to deal with their mistrust issues not me. All I know is that I am not leading him back to Jamaya. Not just yet anyway.

The news she gave me nearly blew me away. Maybe if I talk to the guys and tell them about the baby they would allow her to live at least until the baby is born. Then they can do what they want to do with her.

I know that sounds bad but what else is there for me to do. I love my child already, but how do I know she isn't just telling me that to save her life. I need to find out and I won't be able to do that until I shake this tail I have on me. Damn Isaiah.

I decided to head on home and get some rest it had been a long day, but Jamaya just won't let me rest. She is blowing up my phone nonstop. Why didn't she just listen to me and get as far away from here as possible. I pray to God that she isn't home, and I don't pray at all.

When I got half way home I called Isaiah and told him to pull up behind me so I can give him his truck back. He was quiet for a second. I guess it kind of surprised him that I knew all along that he was following me.

I watched as he pulled up slowly behind me and got out. I was kind of hurt but I wasn't going to let it show. I know where it's coming from so I can't do anything but respect that. I love them and I hope that Jamaya isn't pregnant so I can get this ugly business behind me.

• • •

I stepped out of Isaiah's truck and placed his keys in his hand. I had so much I wanted to say to him but I decided to just let it go. This just wasn't the place or time,

"I guess we even with this gas thing then?" I laughed.

"Yeah we straight." Isaiah replied with a smirk.

I could tell that Isaiah wasn't too happy about the situation but that was the only way I could get him off my ass for a little while.

"You might as well call it a night man. I'm heading to the crib."

"So you don't have anything else planned?"

"Like what Isaiah?"

"I don't know. I was just asking why you so jumpy?"

"I'm not jumpy. You know what I think?"

"What you thinking Cory. Please just fill me."

. . .

130

"I think you're pissed right now that I ain't lead you to Jamaya, but you know what? Follow me for all I care."

"If you think I'm going to stand out here on the side of the road and fuss with you then you're sadly mistaken." Isaiah said with an attitude.

"Good then take your ass home."

The more I stood there and talked to him the more I got mad. I felt betrayed.

I walked passed him and got inside my car and pulled away. He was still standing there when I turned the corner heading toward my house. I hate fighting with my brothers, but this is different because I never fought with Isaiah before. Well nothing like this. We only bumped heads every once in a while. He has always been the peace maker. He's the middle man between us brothers.

I didn't even pull up in my driveway good before he pulled in right behind me. Damn. I'm so tired of this. I didn't even say anything. I just unlocked the front door and left it open so Isaiah could walk inside. I didn't even look around the house. I could tell as soon as I entered that she wasn't here. The feel of the house was different.

Isaiah walked in and walked right passed me. I could hear him walking up the stairs checking room by room. I went in the kitchen and looked for something to eat.

I raised my head and look over the fridge door when he walked through the kitchen.

"What want something to eat?"

"Yeah what you got?"

"Shit nothing I was thinking about ordering a pizza. Is that cool?"

"Sounds good to me; what's in there to drink?"

I pulled out two beers and we headed into the den. We might as well catch up on some sports while we wait. I looked over at Isaiah and started flipping through channels.

Isaiah

I could feel Cory watching me and I knew he's mad, but he was acting strangely and it was beginning to bother me. We have always had misunderstanding but never concerning someone that we loved. I know he is upset, and I could also see that he is hurt about what has taken place over the course of the day. I wanted to stay quiet, but something was telling me that he really needed to talk. He didn't say anything just got up and heading back into the kitchen. I think I'm going to ask him what was on his mind when he returns.

"I'll get it." I jumped up at the sound of the doorbell. I passed Cory on the way from the kitchen with two sodas in hand.

I sat down and opened up the pizza box. The smell of cheese filled the air letting me now that I was past hungry. I almost ate the whole box by myself when

I realized that Cory hadn't eaten anything. Something was definitely on his mind.

"Ok spill it Cory. What the hell is going on with you?"

"Huh, what you mean? It's nothing really."

"Stop lying you know I could always tell when you lie."

"You know that Jamaya has been in contact with me."

"Yeah I know. Do that mean you know where she at?"

"No, I don't know where she at Isaiah. She told me something else that floored me man."

"What did she say?" I rolled my eyes knowing he was about to say some crazy shit.

"It had me thinking and I'm so confused about how I'm going to handle this situation if she is telling me the truth.

"What the hell did she say man? Telling the truth about what?"

"She said that she is pregnant Isaiah?"

"What! You have to be kidding me."

"That's what she said. I couldn't talk to her anymore. I swear Isaiah I don't know where the hell she's at. She had been calling me nonstop except for the past hour or so."

"So you really don't know where she at then?"

"No I don't and if she is carrying my baby then I am glad I didn't kill her earlier."

"Damn how the hell you didn't know this before Cory?"

"Man that girl up the strip so much it's hard to know if her moods change. I wanted to talk to you and Mike about this. It's been on my mind since she told me, but I just don't know if it's true."

"Alright, I'm going to back off and let you handle this and tomorrow we will talk to Mike and fill him in. The next time she calls talk to her and find out where she's at, and for God sake buy a test and test that bitch yourself."

"Thanks for understanding Isaiah, because you just don't believe what was going through my mind. I didn't know what to do to be honest."

"Well we can't solve all our problems over night but we can try." I stood up to leave. I just couldn't take it anymore. This was straight bullshit. I know one thing for sure that she wasn't here. If what she told Cory was true then we have to handle this in another way.

Would Mike understand that? Would he kill her anyways and hurt his brother just because he could. How could this situation get any worse? This is a lot to take in for anybody.

I looked at my watch and noticed that I might as well go home and please my baby. On my way home I was trying to come up with a way to break the news to Mike if she was pregnant.

It took me a minute to get home. The one thing I liked about us is that our homes are in the same area. I will swing by Mike's house tomorrow and check on things there. I haven't been there in about a week.

I pulled in between Erica silver and black BMW and my dark blue and black Changer. I looked at my house and it looked like any other home in the neighborhood. The front door opened and Erica stood there with two glasses of wine in her hands, and all the stress of the day just went away. All I thought about was being with my woman and letting everything else go. As her arms wrapped around me and her kiss started to warm up my body in places only she could. I pushed the front door closed with my feet, scooped her up in my arms and carried her to our bedroom.

Veronica Meek

Chapter 8

Mike

When I opened my eyes this morning I saw the most beautiful woman watching over me. She smiled and I couldn't help but smile back. What had this woman done to me? It's like I'm looking forward just to seeing her. She is so easy to talk to and sometimes I feel like I could spill my soul and she would understand. We talked for hours last night before she had to leave. I had one of the most peaceful sleeps that I have had in years. She eases the pain I have inside. She makes me feel loved. I haven't felt that since my mom died.

Without Makalya around, days seem to pass by instead of hours. I just don't understand why it felt like I knew her all my life. I am learning to open up and love.

She smiles at me and I feel my stomach do flip flops. She places her book down and walks over and places a kiss on my forehead.

"Hey sleepy head I thought you would never wake up."

"Hey baby, I see you're here early this morning. What time is it?"

Makalya looked at her watch, "It's a little after 9 am."

"I'm hungry can you roll that tray over here to me baby. Thank you. Not only are you beautiful but you're sweet too."

I said as I lifted the top off of the food and was surprised to find it still hot. "They must have just brought this in here?"

"Yes about 5 minutes before you woke up."

"I wonder why they were so late bringing it this morning."

"I told them to take it back and let you sleep. You looked so peaceful and I didn't want them to wake you."

"How long have you been here?"

"I don't really know maybe since 5:30 this morning."

"5:30 and why didn't you wake me? Damn baby I'm sorry."

"What are you sorry for? It isn't your fault I couldn't sleep last night."

"I'm so ready to go home. I'm sick and tired of looking at this place."

"Mike can I ask you something?"

"Sure baby you can ask me anything."

"Do you remember what happened to you the night you got shot?"

"Makalya baby what happened that night is between family."

"So, you do remember?"

"Baby all I need is for you to continue doing what you are doing to make me better. That matter is between me and my brothers."

She could tell he was serious about what he was saying and she didn't want to push him. "Ok just understand baby that I'm here to help you."

"You're already helping me enough; I don't know how to thank you or would I ever be able to repay you for all that you have done for me."

Makalya got quiet after that so I started to eat. After I finished I pushed the tray away I slide back my covers and reached down to ease one of my legs over the side of the bed.

"Just what do you think you're doing?"

"I'm going to the bathroom what does it look like?"

"It looks like you about to fall flat on your face that's what."

"I can do this ok."

"You haven't been walking in months Mike. You haven't even started rehab yet."

"So what's that supposed to mean."

"It means if you want to really use the restroom let me call for help."

"I can do this. I'm a man dammit!"

"At least let me help you."

"Damn Makelya what I just say." I never raised my voice at her before but she didn't look surprised in the least. She just put her hands on her hips and stood there watching me. It took so much strength fussing with her I didn't have any left to do what needed to be done, but she will never know it. I ease the other leg over the side of the bed and pushed up on the dresser beside my bed. My body feels like dead weight. I could feel my legs about to buckle.

"See what I mean Mike? You are so hard headed." Makalya said as she ran up and wrapped her arms around my waist. "I told you that you needed help baby. I don't want you to fall and hurt yourself trying to move so fast. Your recovery will take time."

"As much as I love your arms around me baby, I'm just going to have to say this again. I'm a man and I'm not going to let nothing stand in my way of getting my energy and strength back. I have things to do you feel me?"

She didn't say anything as we slowly made it to the bathroom. She tried to lift up my gown but I hit her hand away. "I got this." I looked from her to the door and she just stood there giving me the eye right back.

"I'm not going anywhere so you might as well stop eyeing me." She turned around and gave me as much privacy as she could when standing in that bathroom with me.

I sighed. I didn't even try to stand just lifted up the gown and sat down on the toilet. I knew that moment as Makayla stood there listening to me use the bathroom that I was going to make her my wifey.

Cory

As I lay in bed thinking about my wifey a wave of sadness came over me as things continue to run through my head. I couldn't believe how she broke the number one code within any organized family. How could she have been so stupid? To think she might be carrying my seed really depressed the hell out of me. Jamaya was my wifey in all shape and form and by the street code the only person to take her life was me, and I know my brother's aren't going to let this rest until she is dealt with. They just don't know how much I thought about running away with her, but that's a death sentence for both of us. Well make that all three of us if it's true what she says about the baby.

Jamaya was a hit man's wifey, and she passed the point of no return when she tried to take a member of our family out. I'm still trying to understand what the hell she was thinking, because as far as I know she's never been on the other side of a bullet.

A street code is written in blood and she spilled family blood, so it's only right that she shed hers in return, but the thoughts of our baby flood my dreams as I tried to sleep. I dreamed about my lil man. I could see his brown eyes and his curly black hair. I see his little face so clearly.

As I slept I saw what could have been our lil mama. She had the same little dimple like her mom and the same brown eyes as our lil man, but her hair was long and sandy red just like mine. Then pain torn through my dreams and went straight to my heart when I heard her laugh, but I couldn't wake up. I saw them both playing and laughing and when my lil man fell and hurt his leg. I even heard him cry. I'm dying inside knowing I have to put an end to my family. I know Isaiah said find out if she's pregnant or not and we'll decide what to do then, but I know deep inside I could never trust her again, and if she lives long enough to have our child I have to look at them every day knowing that I'm the one hurting them because I took their mother away.

I wish I could just end all of our pain and suffering now, and the only person that's left to feel any pain would be me. Which I would deserve because I'm the one that brought her into our lives. I reached for my cell phone and placed the call that would change our lives. When I heard the voice on the other end my heart broke and tears started falling once again. It killed me to hear the excitement in her voice.

"Hey baby I have been waiting forever for you to call me back.

"What hotel you at?"

She got quiet and I could tell she was trying to decide could she trust me or not.

"Why?"

"What you mean why, because I wanna know where that's why?"

"How come I can't meet you somewhere in public?"

"Don't play with me Jamaya. Now I'm gonna ask you again; where you at? Do you really think I'll hurt my own damn baby?" I yelled.

"I don't know really. How could I know if your brothers haven't turned you totally against me?"

"You don't know that, but you should have thought of that before you were calling me like you were crazy. I told you to run so now deal with it."

"I could have left without telling you about the baby?"

"Where are you?" I raised my voice again letting her no I didn't have time for this shit.

Jamaya sighed. "I'm downtown at the Hilton."

"Oh now you trying to be funny; what room are you in?"

"I'm in room 316."

"I'm on my way."

"Could you bring me something···"

I hung up the phone I didn't care what else she had to say. It didn't matter I got what I wanted out of her ass. I looked over at the clock sitting on the dresser and it said 1:45 in the morning. I should at least try and get some more sleep, but what's the use I know for now on that my dreams are going to be hunted.

I laid there looking off in space and the next time I looked over at the clock it was only 2:30.

"Damn I'm not going to get any sleep I might as well get the hell up."

I can't sleep in this bed without her. Hell I can't stand to be in this house without her. Just to think as we shared this bed this morning that my girl had a knife buried deep in my back.

Isaiah

I didn't get much sleep last night. I had Cory's situation on my mind. What if she is carrying his baby? There's no way he would take care of her now. I just couldn't wait any longer to talk to Mike. We had to figure this out and soon, because I don't know what Cory would do.

I pulled up to the hospital a little after 10 in the morning with a hot breakfast in hand. I know Mike would love some real food for a change. I stopped in the hall and got and update from the doctor and then headed inside of Mike's room.

I heard Mike in the bathroom, and it sounded like he was getting out the shower. He was talking to somebody and whatever he said had the female help laughing. Yeah big bro always had a way with the women.

I moved his empty tray to the table by the wall and placed his hotcakes and sausages on it along with an OJ. I didn't even look up when the bathroom door opened and they slowly walked out, but when I turned around I got the surprise of my life.

"What the hell?" I said out loud.

Both the doctor and Mike looked over at me.

"What?" they said in unison.

"Nothing." I sat the bag of food down and walked back over to the room door.

When I looked out I saw the doctor still standing in the hall talking to the other doctors. She smiled and I smiled back and close the room door again. I turned around and stood there with my arms crossed.

I watched as she helped Mike back in bed and pulled the tray close to him.

"You know you just finished eating."

"And. This here is better." Mike said as he looked up at me smiling. "Thanks bro."

I couldn't say anything I just continued to stand there.

"Is something wrong Isaiah?" She asked.

"Yes as a matter of fact it is?" I said as I walked up to her.

She didn't even try to bag back. "What is it?"

"Just who the hell are you?"

"What?"

"What going on Isaiah you know who she is?" Mike said looking confused.

"I said who the hell are you?"

"Isaiah man this is crazy now what's going on?" Mike asked this time he was getting a little upset.

"Maybe you need to ask your girlfriend here."

She didn't say a word as both of the brothers turned their eyes on her. She reached inside of her back pants pocket and pulled out a FBI badge and showed it to us.

"What the hell? So that what all the questions was about this morning?" Mike said.

"What questions?"

"She asked me if I knew what happened on the day I was shot."

"So Ms. FBI Agent tell me what the Feds have to do with my brother?"

"I would like to talk to Mike first if you don't mind."

"Well as you see I do mind. What do he have to do with y'all?"

"He doesn't have anything to do with the Feds this is other business."

"Other business like what?" Mike asked as he pushed his plate away there was no way he could eat now.

"I also work for the Southside Mafia Family."

"What? So you telling me Sam is the one that sent you?" Mike said sounding surprised.

"What the hell. So now Sam doesn't trust us when it comes to you Mike? That's what it sounds like to me."

"Okay guys let me start at the beginning please just calm down. My name isn't Makayla that's my twin sister's name. My name is just Kayla."

"Wait a minute." Mike stopped her. "Isaiah how did you know something wasn't right here?"

"I just was talking to the doctor in the hall way that's how I knew."

"Well damn. Ok Kayla go ahead." Mike laid his head down on his pillow like he was just worn out.

"Like I was saying my name is Kayla and every since you been here I been watching over you when I have some free time. It was hard getting my sister to go along with this but she owes my big time."

"How does she owes you like that knowing she could lose her job if anyone finds out what you two were doing?" I asked.

"If it wasn't for me she wouldn't be a doctor that's how. I worked my ass off coming up with the money for school, and that's how I ended up working with Sam."

"So you knew all along what we did for a living? What about your sister?"

"No she doesn't know nothing and we going to keep it that way. She just thinks I have a thing for Mike that's all."

"So you were using me pumping me for information?" Mike asked and you could hear the hurt in his voice.

"No baby that wasn't what I was doing. I am feeling you. I even told Sam that something was happening with us."

"What did he say?" Mike asked rising his head up a little bit more.

"He just told me to be careful and that if you get your memory back that you would be one tough pistol." She laughed. "But I told him not to worry I can handle you."

"Mike I can't believe you sitting here listening to this shit. This bitch got your head wide open."

"It's all true if you don't believe me call Sam and he can clear everything up."

"Don't worry your pretty little head Agent I am." I said as I pulled my cell out and walked out the room. "

Aint this some shit? I didn't even get a chance to talk to Mike about Cory ass yet." I said to myself as Sam picked up the phone.

*C*hapter 9

Mike

I was speechless. I wanted so much to ask her more questions, but I just didn't know where to start. I closed my eyes and tried to take all of this in because I knew what I just heard couldn't be true. I can't be with a FBI Agent and she couldn't be with me. It just wouldn't work. I was already having doubts about her but now I know it's just isn't happening.

"So you're not going to say nothing at all huh?" Kayla asked.

"What's to say really? You played me for a fool that's all so I guess you have the last laugh anyway."

"I didn't play you for a fool Mike. I want you and I'm going to have you case closed."

"I'm not one of those people you can just boss around because you carry a badge."

"I know who you are and I always have, so don't lay there trying to talk yourself out of being with me."

"It was never us Kayla or Makayla whatever your damn name is."

"So you're going to walk away from what we have?"

"What we had was based on a lie so I don't have to walk away from something that wasn't there."

"How could you say that?"

I looked at her and I saw tears in her eyes, but what she didn't know was that don't faze me. She could cry from now to dooms day and it wouldn't change the fact she had lied to me. If she lied once she would do it again point blank. So I laid there and said nothing.

• • •

"I can't believe you Mike this isn't over."

"So now you're going to threatening me."

"I'm not threatening you. I love you." She yelled.

"What, you don't even hardly know me so what are you talking about. You love me. Yeah right."

"Look at me Mike and tell me you don't feel the same way."

I wouldn't look at her. Hell I couldn't because I have some very strong feeling for this woman and it could very well be love. I know what's best for me and that is to walk away now before things get too out of hand with her.

"What, you not talking to me now?"

"There is nothing to say. Just go Kayla."

"No, I'm not going anywhere. I know you love me like I love you and I am not going to walk away from you."

She walked over to me and turned my face toward hers, and she kissed me. I mean really kissed me. It wasn't like anything I ever felt before. I knew she put her heart and soul into that kiss. I wrapped my arms around her and pulled her closer until she was damn near on top of me.

I knew she loved me and I loved her, but I can't for the life of me let her go. I kissed her back with as much passion she gave out, and I didn't let her up until I felt one of her tears fall on my face.

"Don't cry baby." I said as I wiped away her tears. "I'm not going anywhere. As of today you're my wifey and you're mine."

"Oh Mike. Promise me you want leave me baby. I wouldn't be able to take it if you do."

"I don't have to promise anything because you have my heart and I'm not going to go too far without it."

"I never left your side since the first day you came here."

"I know baby, I know you been here and I can't walk away from someone that sat beside my bed and cried day after day praying for me to get better."

"How you know I did that?"

"I remember everything even when I wasn't all the way awake. I remember you calling my name. I remember you kissing my softly on my lips as you came and went. I remember when you used to sing to me."

She smiled. "Oh God I was hoping you didn't remember all that."

"Why baby?"

"Because I can't sing that's why." They laughed.

"Yeah you right about that but I looked forward to hearing it anyway."

I pulled her close again and I just held her. I couldn't let her go and I won't, and that's the way Isaiah found us when he came back inside the room.

Cory

I pulled into Wal-Mart because this was the only place close to her that was open this time of morning. I had to get a pregnancy test. I needed to know was she carrying my seed or not. Even though I still have a hundred and one reasons to stop this madness and just be the man that I am supposed to be.

I think it would be easier to kill her and not even think about if she's pregnant with my child or not. I know it would be taken the easy way out for not knowing if I killed my own child or not. Once I made my mind up I was in and out of the store within ten minutes. I have 3 different kinds of tests in hand, but I'm still torn.

I parked down the street from the hotel. I was dressed in all black. I had on a black hoodie and some black Guess jeans and black Tim's. As I walked through the parking lot I spotted her

Green Land Rover parked up front in the VIP parking lot. It's just like her no matter how much shit she's in she still did things in style.

When I walked through the front door of the hotel the man at the front desk stopped what he was doing and started to watch me like I was about to steal something, but I continue to walk. I didn't even look his way, but I saw the look he was giving me out the corner of my eyes. I pushed the elevator button and the doors open right up. I step inside and hit 3 for the 3rd floor.

My heart was beating fast. I wanted to see my girl again. I loved her. I wanted to lie in her arms and let her hold me. The doors opened and I stepped off the elevator. I looked at the signs that show which way was room 316 and headed in that direction.

I stopped in front of her door and I could smell her all the way out in the hallway. Her Chanel No. 5 wrapped around my heart and squeezed. I closed my eyes trying hard to control my breathing. I knocked on the door. Tap. Tap. It wasn't a loud knock just loud enough not to draw attention to myself. I could hear her moving around and my palms started to sweat. I wiped my hands on my jeans and waited until she opened the door.

She pulls the door open slowly. I couldn't see her but I knew she was there. I didn't move I just stood there in the hallway wondering why she was hiding behind the door. I knew she was scared and she had every right to be.

"Why you hiding behind the door Jamaya is someone else in there with you?" I said through the opening. I still didn't make a move.

She opened the door on up. "No why in the world would someone else be here? Now you're the one talking crazy."

I walked passed her and check the hotel suite. She just stood there watching me, but I didn't trust her anymore and that was just plain and simple.

"I wanted you to bring me something to eat but you hung up before I could get it out my mouth." She said as she looked at the bag I had in my hand. "Why you go to Waymart? What you got in there?"

"Here" I handed her the bag. She looked inside and I could tell that she wasn't happy to see the home pregnancy tests.

"Why you brought this? I already told you I was pregnant. What is this you don't believe me?"

"Hell naw! I don't believe a word that comes out your lying ass mouth girl." I grabbed the bag back and took the box out and opened it. "Here lets go I want to see you take this."

"I don't have to use it now."

"Does it look like you have an option right now Jamaya?"

She walks over to me with tears in her eyes. It killed me to see how much she is hurting behind this, but she brought it all down on herself. "What the hell was she thinking?" I put the bag down on the table next to the bed and let her walk into my arms. I knew she needed to be held. Hell so did I. I put my hand on the base of her head and gently laid it down on my shoulder. I just held her while she cried.

I didn't want to let her go but this shit weight heavy on my mind, I needed to know was she carrying my child or not.

"Baby I don't want to rush, but I just need to know. Go take the test."

She lifted her head up and gave me a look like she hated me so much right now for not believing her. She walked over to the mini fridge and got out a bottle of water. Then she walked over and got one of the tests out the bag and heading for the rest room. When she started to close the door I put my hands out to stop it.

"Just what do you think you are doing Cory? Don't tell me you are going to watch me take this."

"Damn right I am. I don't know why you looking so damn shocked."

"You gonna watch my piss?"

"Yes are you hard of hearing or something? You ain't been having a problem with me watching you before."

I took the box from her and opened it up and pulled the little cup out.

"Here" I said as I handed her the cup that was inside. I stood there waiting; listening but not one sound came from her. "What the hell taking so long?"

"I already told you before I didn't have to go, but you didn't listen to me."

I walked over to the sink and turn the water on. "Now that should help."

"Here and I hope you happy." She raised the cup up with a little pee inside.

"Yea I am." I said and walked out with the cup in my hand. I placed it down in the table and read the instructions that

I pulled from the box. I look back inside and pulled out a strip and placed it inside the little cup for a few seconds. Now all we have to do now is wait, and she better pray to God that it isn't negative because if I find out she been lying to me again I'm going to break her fucking neck.

Jamaya

I sat in the bathroom trying to get myself together. I already knew the results but it still scared the hell out of me that Cory didn't trust me anymore. He was so quiet in there and somehow I felt like an animal being preyed upon.

I turned the water on deciding to take a hot bath. I wasn't scared about the baby. I was scared because without it I would have been dead right now.

I have done some crazy shit in my time but this here is by far the worse. I had things all planned out and now I'm stuck with a child I don't want in order to save my life. I'm glad I didn't get an adoption like I started too , and the only thing that stopped me was that my emotions were playing with me. That's what happens when you fall in love.

I stepped out of my night gown and sat down inside the warm water letting it wrap around my body. I closed my eyes as the sweet smell of vanilla totally relaxed me and that is how I was when Cory walked in.

"Wake up baby."

"Huh."

"Wake up you fell asleep."

"Oh. I just have been so tired lately." That was when I felt how cool the water had gotten. "How long have I been in here?"

"A little over 30 minutes that's all."

"Oh ok. I'm just ready to go to sleep." I got out and stood there as Cory dried me off. I felt like I was dead on my feet. These last few days had done a number on me.

"Come on let's go to bed."

"You mean you're staying?"

"Yes baby I'm staying. I can't sleep without you."

"Oh Cory." I said as I went into his arms. He lifted me up and carried me out of the bathroom. "I knew I could count on you."

"Jamaya now you already know if it wasn't for this baby thing, things wouldn't be like this."

"I know and that's why I'm happy because you didn't have to listen to a thing that I said, but I'm show glad that you did. Get some sleep I really don't want to talk about this anymore."

Cory set me down softly on the bed and begins to undress and then got into the bed next to me. When I eased under him he pulled the covers up over us.

"Cory."

"Hmm,"

"I love you."

"And I love you too baby girl."

I closed my eyes and smiled when I felt Cory place his hand on my stomach. Now this is the way it was supposed to be just the 3 of us. I have to come up with some way to get him to leave Atlanta with me.

As sleep claimed me once again a little voice said, "It will be a cold day in hell before you pull him away from his brother's."

I pushed that to the back of my mind as I turned into my baby embrace and softly said, "Then I'm going to die trying because he's mine."

A Brother's Bond

There have been times in our lives that

We had our ups and downs.

I have been pulled between

Both brothers'

And still held my ground.

I watched over one brother

Until he was awake.

And watch the other one decides

On a life to take.

There is one thing that

Would never change.

No matter how deep we

Are in this game

We have a brother's bond.

Even tho we live our lives

By the guns.

Isaiah

If I haven't been living through these months I would have believed I was dreaming. I feel like someone was going to punch me at any moment and I'm going to wake up. How in the world could our family be this far gone? Am I the only once left that has any sense at all?

What I know is that business didn't come to a stop when one of the best hit men was laid up in the hospital. Hundreds of calls continued to come even though they knew that Mike wasn't able to still handle business. Business is Business no matter what is going on in your life.

Once again my phoned buzzed in my pocket; no matter how much I wanted to just let it ring I still knew that business had to continue.

"Sam I'm surprised to hear from you so soon." I said into my cell.

"As you know my friend time is money."

"Yes I know, so tell me what you got for me?"

"You know I hate to take you from your brother side, but we need to meet as soon as possible."

"This sounds serious."

"It is. How soon can you meet up with me?"

"Just give me the time and place and I'm there."

"Well give me an hour and I'll hit you on the hip with the location."

"I got you Sam."

Now I couldn't help but wonder what in the world is going on now. Sam has been nothing but great to us since we first started this business. Hell if it wasn't for him we wouldn't be in this line of work at all.

That's why it kind of hurt me to know that he had sent someone to watch over Mike. I wasn't no fool and either was Mike. The only reason Sam sent her was to see if Mike had become one of his weak links.

I know deep down in my heart she would have killed him if she had too, and she still might. I don't know what it will take for Mike to see that it's something about her, but he's blinded by what he thinks is love.

She had been looking over our shoulders for months now and even her sister is riding on my "Going to get your ass" list right now. I just don't understand why he doesn't see that that is a sign of betrayal for what she had done.

It looks like I'm the only one out of the 3 of us that isn't stuck on pussy right now. What I do know is that they need to get their women under control before they be their down fall.

Gangsta Killers

Chapter 10

Mike

The day seems to be moving fast to me, but that always happen when I'm with Kayla. She hasn't left my side at all today. I was happy to see that she felt comfortable around me. I mean so comfortable that she asked her job to fax her some papers because she was going to take some time off of work. I couldn't believe she was doing all of this for me. I needed to make her understand that she needed to be as far away from me as possible.

"I think you should leave Kayla."

"Mike we just been through this why do you want to send me away? Don't you see that I'm in love with you?"

"All I see is that I'm no good for you."

"How could you say that?"

"Why is it so hard for you to see that it's true? You need someone and something good in your life. Not someone like me."

She looked at me as her eyes glazed over with tears.

"And what's wrong with you huh? Tell me Mike. What... you don't need love like everyone else?"

"I'm not saying that."

"Right now I don't give a fuck what you are saying. I'm here and I'm not going anywhere. So that mean you need to deal with it."

With every word she said her eyes shot sharks at me and I knew she meant ever word she said. How could I turn my back on her when I knew I meant so much to her. I'm just finding it hard to believe that she really does love me. I could see by looking at her that this was going to hurt me more than it is going to hurt her; so I turned my back to her, and didn't say another word.

"So you just going to turn your back on me?"

Still I didn't say anything there wasn't nothing left to say. I'm her past as of right now and she needs to start a future with someone better than me.

"Mike please don't do this we can make this work!" Kayla begged.

Still silent I laid there with my back to her until I heard her leave the room. My heart ached uncontrollably. I was in so much pain I couldn't even move. It was easier to lay here and let the best thing I ever had walk out of my life. I know God placed her here to better me; make me a better man, and help me change my life around. But I don't deserve anyone like her and I never will. I turned back around slowly I was dying inside knowing I just let the best thing walk out of my life.

But there she was standing before me naked, proud and magnificently beautiful. I became aroused to a point that it hurt. How I wish I could see her like that every day of my life. She walked toward me tall and sexy, and not one thing out of place on her body. My eyes were glued to her face and slowly moving down her body. My body reacted with a force that almost had me shaken. Damn, I wanted her so badly.

She reached down and pulled the covers off of my body, which was already alive and ready. All I had on was my hospital gown which made it easy for my manhood to stand up in the air. I clenched my hands closed trying hard not to touch her. She smiled. Then she shoved my gown up and with her fingers she begins to caress and massage a place that hasn't been touch in a long time.

I moaned. "Oh God baby why you doing this to me?"

"Are you convinced now that I want you? That I need you, and most importantly that I love you."

My breathing was uncontrollable as her fingers moved rhythmically up and down my manhood. I couldn't speak so I moved my head from side to side just enjoying this wonderful feeling. It got to a point that I couldn't help myself so I begged her to just take me right then and there. She lowered her head and touched her tongue where her fingers were just moments ago.

"Kayla."

It was so hard to contain myself as her mouth closed over my manhood. The warmness of her mouth felt like magic. She had me grabbing the covers like I was the woman. I laid by with my eyes closed as she moved her mouth up and down. I could feel myself close to the edge and she knew it too.

She stopped and placed little kisses up and down my chest. She didn't stop kissing me until she was totally on top of me. I look her in her eyes as she placed me inside of her. She was tight and wet. She slides down on me slowly. My head started spinning and my eyes started rolling to the back of my head.

I reached behind and cupped her. I needed her to meet my every thrust. Her head went back and our speed increased. I became more forceful with every movement. She cried out and lay limp on my chest.

"I love you too baby." She heard me say as we both drifted off to sleep.

Cory

I knew this was the right thing to do as soon as I walked through the door and saw the scared look on her face. Now I am laying here with my hand place on her stomach when it finally hit me that I could never hurt my child. That is a part of me growing inside of her. Apart of me that I love very much and I never laid eyes on it. I don't know how long I laid there watching her sleep. I can't even remember the last time I had done it. She looks so peaceful and so beautiful it's so hard to believe that she has a heart as cold as mine.

I don't even know how this child would be affected by the way we live. Its father is a contact killer and its mother ··· well who would even know what would come of her. As of today things have to change between us. I could never trust her again that's for damn sure. I love her, but love just isn't enough.

I pulled her close enjoying the feel of her body next to mine. I'm trying to put all this moment to memory, because I'll never know when this will end. I am glad about one thing though. I get to watch the woman I love grow heavy with our child. I'll get to lay my head on her stomach and listen to the baby heartbeat. I'll get to feel his or her little kicks against my hands. Hell naw, I'm not going to let her take that away from me. Until today I never knew I wanted to be a father until I saw the positive sign on that stick. I never look past the fact that it would always be just me and my brothers. So much has change and I got to make it right, but how can I fix her wrong?

I will never truly know why she did the things that she did. You just don't do things like that to family and she was part of ours rather she knew it or not. Damn fool.

The anger set in along with all the hurt and I know that it's going to be hard to let things chill. How could you love someone and hate them at the same time? That's what's going through my mind right now. Wheels are turning in my head should I kill her now and take a chance of not seeing or knowing my baby? Or wait and see if she'll pull something else like this again. Maybe next times she will succeed. I'm stuck between a rock in a hard place. I'm totally lost.

I closed my eyes willing myself to get some sleep, and try to relax and just let things unfold day by day. Dealing with someone like her makes me wonder today might be my last day. She did try to have Mike killed and I know if she's afraid enough she just might try to kill me.

Of course she's afraid for her life, and she should be. What I'm going through would drive any sane man to drink and have many sleepless nights.

Isaiah

It didn't seem like an hour had passed before Sam called me again.

"Isaiah I need you to meet me somewhere. Is that possible?"

"Are you talking about right now?"

"Yes the sooner the better."

"Sam what's going on? I never heard you sound like this before."

"Like I said when we talked earlier I'll have to tell you this in person. Meet me in 10 minutes at Jack's downtown."

"Okay I'll meet you there. Do you need me to have Cory meet us there too?"

"No I need only you, and Isaiah this is very important so that means it's only between me and you."

"I'm on my way."

After I hang up with him my mind went into over drive. What could have happened to make the head of one of the largest mafia families turn to me. I think someone could have finally put Sam in his place. Only time would tell.

I'm sitting in traffic on 75 south; Atlanta traffic is the worse. I couldn't help but think that maybe this could help Mike and get that agent off his back if I could get to the bottom of what's going on with Sam. This has to be something personal to him because he never wanted to meet when it comes to handling business. I have always dealt with his son Big B.

Sam's family has thrown a lot of work our way because he doesn't want his sons to go down for murder, and that reason alone is why we make the big bucks.

Damn this is really driving me crazy not knowing what's happening with Sam. I don't want to walk into anything blind. I'll never know what Sam has planned now that Mike is out of commission.

He's a good guy and all, but my life is just as important as his sons. Something keeps telling me to fill my brothers in on what's going on right now, but both their heads stuck so far up those bitches asses it's just stupid crazy.

I pulled into Jack's parking lot with two minutes left to spare. I took that time and watched my surroundings. A few seconds later Sam pulls into the parking lot in a mint green Jaguar. I continued to sit there and watch making sure no funny shit was about to go down.

Sam got out his car; hit the alarm and headed for the restaurant door. He stopped looked around, looked down and checked his watch.

I couldn't help but admire the man he had everything I wanted. He had the women, money, and a nice size family that he could call his own. Sometimes I wonder if any of us will be around long enough to have all those things. Well at least Cory has stated making his family even if the bitch wouldn't be around long enough to enjoy it.

Come to think about it I haven't heard from Cory all day. When I finish with this meeting with Sam I'm going to hit him up if he hasn't contacted me by then.

I looked around one more time deciding it was safe; opened up my truck door, and stepped out into the warm afternoon sunshine.

Gangsta Killers

Chapter 11

Mike

Therapy was hell and there is nothing in the world I want to get over more than anything is this weakness. I know I pushed myself too hard today, but I just didn't care. I have someone waiting on me and that's something I never had before. I'm ready to go home. I know I'm well enough to do so too, but my baby and her twin just fuss over me. It makes me feel so special.

I know my brothers aren't going to agree with my relationship with Kayla, but I'm not going to let that faze me. They just don't see what I see, and they have to realize the fact that she has been here for me all this time just like they have. I only hope she could deal with the real me; the person that I really am. I'm not this weak little man that she came to love. I'm a killer; A gangsta killer. That's what I do and that will never change.

How could she honor her badge and me too? I don't truly know but I'm going to find out. This isn't a game she walking into. I had been trying to protect her from me, the real me, and this life. I have to make it known that if she's going to be down with me then she needs to know that she would be down for life. There is only one way of leaving me and I know she want be leaving it walking.

I picked up the remote control wanting to see what's on. I wanted to catch up on the news, but I still have a few hours before it comes on. I flipped through the channels a few times and stopped on the first channel that looked like it was showing something worth watching.

I closed my eyes for a few minutes, because I felt a headache coming on.

"I just know you ain't in here watching Lifetime?"

My eyes popped open. I knew this bitch couldn't be standing in my room talking to me. I blinked my eyes. I knew this couldn't be real.

"Yes it's me Mike don't be so shocked."

If I could have gotten up out of bed I would have been over there choking the hell out her, but I have to keep control. I will not let her see what she turned me into.

"What you doing here Jamaya?"

She smiled could you believe this. She had to know I got me memory back.

"How are you feeling Mike?"

"Are you hard of hearing I asked you why are you here?"

"I came to see how you were. Why else would I be here?"

"Where is Cory?"

"He was sleep when I last saw him. Why you need me to call him for you?"

"Cut the fucking bullshit."

"Mike I know you're mad."

"Mad, bitch I'm past mad."

"And you should be. I know that saying I'm sorry isn't going to change the way you feel about me."

"You think."

"Can we please try to work things out?"

"There isn't anything to work out."

"But⋯"

"But nothing Jamaya. You tried to have me killed twice."

"But Mike what about my baby?"

"What baby? What the hell you talking about?"

"You don't know? I mean Cory didn't tell you?"

"Don't you think if I knew I wouldn't be asking you what baby?

"I'm having Cory's baby, and I want to be here for our child."

"Be here for your child? Now you lost me."

"I'm not crazy. I know as soon as I give birth Cory is gonna kill me."

"And who told you that?"

"No one didn't have to tell me I just know."

"Jamaya what you want me to do?"

"I want you to talk to Cory. I don't want to die."

"And you think I did?"

"I'm sorry Mike. You'll never no how much I regret what I did."

"Well I'm sorry I can't help you. You're Cory's problem and whatever he decides to do with you is on him."

"Mike you can stop all this with one word."

"Guess what Jamaya? It ain't happening. I don't give a fuck, and when he does lay you down I won't drop a tear. You know what the worse part about all this is that your baby won't either. Now get the hell out my room."

I don't know if Jamaya ever saw hatred before but she just got a taste of it then.

Jamaya

When I left Mike's hospital room I was broken and my heart could never be repaired. How could I believe that I could face him and make a plea for my life? Or that it would turn out any different than what it is now. I was pulling at straws hoping he would feel a little something for me other than hate. Man I was wrong. I stopped outside his room so shaken by my encounter with him that I cried. I laid my head back on the wall and I let it all out. Everything that I had been feeling and had balled up inside of me since all of this started.

"Baby what are you doing here?"

I was so upset that I didn't even hear him walk up.

"Oh Cory." I ran into his arms. "I made a big mistake."

"What did you do Jamaya?"

"I tried to talk to him. I had to let him know that I was sorry. I had to make him understand that I made a huge mistake."

"You shouldn't have come here are you crazy? What if he was strong enough? Don't you know that he would have killed you?"

"The way he just looked at me; I believe you."

"I haven't told him about the baby yet. What if things would have turned out bad? Why didn't you talk to me first?"

"I know you haven't told him, but he knows now. I couldn't talk to you about this. This was something I had to do myself. I got myself into this mess, and it's only fair that I tried to get myself out."

I started to feel a little dizzy and my head started to spin. I felt Cory wrap his arms around me tighter.

"Have you eaten anything today?"

"No, I couldn't eat. I had to try and fix things."

"Don't you see there's nothing you can do the damage has been done. Go get something to eat and get you things from the hotel. I'll meet you at home tonight."

"Okay baby." I kissed him and held him a little longer. "I love you baby."

"I love you too."

I stood there long after he walked into Mike's room. I know now that he's right there nothing else to be done. I'm alive now. I have to stay on Cory good side so I can stay that way.

I was past stressed out when I picked up something to eat and I headed back to the hotel. I put on some little shorts and a tee shirt and headed down to the hot tub. It was time to let the hot stream relax me. It was way past due.

I eased in the hot water and felt my skin sting a little until my body got used to the hot water. I sat down and closed my eyes letting the warm water work its magic.

I relaxed for about an hour and then got all my things together so I could go back home. I think I'll stop by the store and fix Cory his favorite dinner tonight. I know he would love it. I might even get my hair and nails done and pick up a new outfit.

I rush around the room while putting everything back in bags. I called for the valet to come up. It wasn't long before he arrived. I followed him down to the checkout desk only to learn that Cory had already taken care of the bill.

Cory

When I stepped out the elevator Jamaya was the last person I expected to see standing outside of Mike's hospital room. I don't know what between her and Mike, but I could tell it hurt her bad. When I walked inside of his room he was pushing the help button calling for his nurse.

"Mike what's wrong? Do you need me to go get you someone?"

"No they'll be here in a minute."

"I just ran into Jamaya in the hallway."

"Oh yeah."

"Yeah, what happened in here?"

"You mean you didn't ask her?"

"Well no. She was too busy crying."

"That's all you have to say?" I asked Mike.

"What you want me to say Cory?"

"I just want to know what she said to you."

"She came to say that she was sorry."

"That she's sorry?"

"Yeah."

Man it's like pulling teeth with him. Hell I was glad to see the nurse walk in carrying medication. Maybe if he gets something in his system for pain he would be more open, but I know what he's thinking. I'm not crazy and neither is he. I couldn't believe he really thought that I sent her here.

Once he popped his pills he wouldn't even look at me. How could he think the worse of me?

"You think I sent her here don't you?"

"Didn't you? And this baby thing now that was just priceless."

"Mike she really is pregnant."

"What are you serious?"

"Very much so I tested the bitch myself."

"Damn. Well I might as well tell you what's going on."

"What's going on? What you mean by that?"

"You know that the doctor and I are getting close right?"

"Yeah I saw that." I smiled.

"Well how can I say this?"

"Say what?"

"Well most of the time that wasn't the doctor in here with me."

"Huh. I don't understand."

"The doctor has a twin, and the twin name is Kayla she's the one that's been here with me."

"Okay now I'm still lost."

"Makayla is the doctor and Kayla is a FBI Agent."

"FBI Agent, We got the Feds down on us?"

"No we don't. Calm down man. Sam sent her to look after me."

"Sam, what the hell he did some shit like that for? Wait a minute. Are you saying if you woke up talking she was here to finish the job that Jamaya started? Is that what you saying?"

"Something like that."

"Why do I have a feeling there's more?"

"Cause it is."

"Man I need to take a seat." I pulled a chair up to his bed, because I didn't want to miss a word. "Okay go ahead."

"Kayla is my girl now."

"Wow pump yo brakes. You can't be serious?"

"Yes I am."

"Mike you can't do this. You know what we do for a living."

"And so does she."

"I can't believe this shit. What did Isaiah say?"

"He got mad and left."

"Hell I can see why."

"I know this same crazy shit, but I'm feeling her."

"I got you. I know how it feels to have your nose wide open."

They both laughed. "I know what she done isn't forgivable and I'm not expecting you too, you feel me?"

"You damn right it isn't, but I know you love her and you'll love y'all baby too, just like I will love the little killer."

"So you ok with the decision I made concerning Jamaya?"

"Look Cory as long as I don't have to look in her face it's cool with me."

"Thanks man because I didn't know if I had the heart to hurt my baby."

"Cory I wouldn't have let you make that choice in the first place to do something like that anyway, but know one thing though."

"What's that?"

"If a snake bit you once it will do it again."

There wasn't anything left to say on that subject. As of now I had my brother blessing to keep my family.

Whatever this so call doctor/ FBI agent did to him it showed itself today. He must really do be in love.

Isaiah

I set at the table listening while Sam was explaining things to me, and I was shocked about the outcome of that whole situation. It had me wondering how something like that could have happened up under his nose.

Sam turned his cold eyes on me. "Isaiah she been missing all day."

"Are you sure she missing Sam? Maybe she's with some of her friends."

"You don't think I thought of that. I can't half worry about her because my boys are going crazy. They're out for blood right now."

"Damn and what you need from me?"

"I know this isn't your line of work but I need you to keep an eye out for Brian. I'll pay anything you just name it."

"Sam, Brian is more deadly than I am."

"I know, but he isn't thinking clearly right now, and one of Tony's goons could easily take him out. He would do anything to get back at me."

"I see where you going with that, don't worry I got you."

"Thanks Isaiah and this thing with Mike..."

I cut him off. "I understood why you did what you did; a lot of people deal with us, and I know you were only protecting your clients."

"Yeah, I had to have something to tell them you know. It's takes a lot to lock down a City as big as Atlanta."

"I know there's no hard feeling Sam, but I do want to know about this fucking FBI Agent you sent right to our front door."

"You talking about Kayla?"

"Yeah, what's her story?"

"She real folks believe me if I didn't trust her she wouldn't be there. I couldn't believe it when she told me that she and Mike are together now."

"Yeah that's what it looks like, and I'm not feeling this shit at all."

"Kayla is good you feel me. What you need to do is fix that problem you have with Cory. What is this bitch still doing walking?"

"It's a long story."

"I got time."

"I'm going to make a long story short; she's with child."

"You got to be kidding me."

"I wish I was."

"Damn have Cory made his mind up what he going do with her?"

"I haven't heard from him today."

"Well keep me posted on both subjects you feel me, and I'll get back with you soon."

I continued to sit there. My mind went from Cory to Mike and then back to Sam's little problem as I watched him walked out of Jack's. I pulled my cell out and called Mike to see if he heard anything from Cory today. While I'm here I might as see if he wanted something to eat.

"Yeah get me something, and Cory is right here. Why you want him?"

"Naw I just haven't heard from him today. Ask him do he want something too."

"Yeah he'll want something too. It's so funny because he was about to go grab us something."

"Oh well I got y'all. I'll be there in about an hour."

I hung up and order their food and a beer for me while I waited. I keep my eyes on the front door and saw that Sam hasn't pulled out the parking lot yet. Now that really makes me wonder was there more he wasn't telling me.

Chapter 12

Mike

9 months later

No matter how I tried things never did go back to the way they were. My relationship grew with Kayla, and I continued to have a relationship with Cory as long as he didn't bring Jamaya around.

It was hard at first because he wanted me to share in that special part of his life concerning his son, but I couldn't stand the sight of Jamaya.

As the months went I grew stronger she got bigger, but the hatred I felt inside wouldn't go away. Sometimes I sit outside of Cory's house just waiting for the time to strike and take my revenge.

I know Cory prayed that I could move past all of this, but how could I when the woman tried to have me killed not once but twice.

Now that their little man is being born today the time has come to finally see an end to our problems. I waited patiently at the hospital with my brothers waiting to see the new addition to our little family. Of course I'm excited like the next person concerning Cory's son, but it still doesn't change the fact that she's got to go.

Cory's voice brought me back to the present.

"Come on everyone Lil' Cory is finally here." Cory said excitedly.

"Damn about time lil bro. It was looking like his big head wasn't going to never come out." Isaiah said jokingly.

"Baby don't be so mean and you of all people can't talk about no one's head." Erica replied.

The whole waiting room laughed. We really felt like a family, and I didn't want to be the cause of any negative feeling so I relaxed and let the moment take over.

The last thing I want is for anyone pointing their fingers at me saying anything at all about the way I'm acting. I gotten through it this far I can wait a little longer.

"Mike is you coming inside, baby?" Kayla asked.

"Why wouldn't I be; you know I have to see our little man sweetie." I put on the fake smile.

"Are you sure Mike you know we can bring him out so you can see him? I know you don't really want to be around her. I have always kept her away like you asked of me. I don't want you or her to feel uncomfortable. You feel me?" Cory asks.

From the look on his face he was serious and I know he had been trying hard to make both sides of his family happy.

"Cory it's cool what's in the past is in the past. This little baby joined us together as a family, and it's nothing more I wouldn't do to please my family even if it is being around Jamaya for a few minutes. It isn't like I'm moving in with her for God sakes." I laughed trying to lighten the mood.

"You're right I'm sorry big bro. You know I'm just trying to do the right thing."

"Yeah lil bro I know. Now come on and take me to see my little nephew."

I smiled and for the first time in a long time it was a smile of love, because I really do love my bro and his little baby. I wouldn't want to mess up his special day by being an ass. He had been down with me through all of my pains, and now it's time for me to push mine away if only for a while.

Yes I'm going to go face the lion, but what she doesn't know she is going to look into the eyes of a beast. A beast she's going to have to face one day real soon.

Jamaya

I was so tired and it felt like my body was drained. I knew giving birth was going to be hard, but I didn't know it would take so much from you. I couldn't help but think about the family out there waiting to see my baby boy. I wish I could just sleep because my body was totally out of it.

When I held him for the first time I never knew I could feel this way about another person or that I would feel this kind of love. I believed that I loved Cory but his love wasn't nothing compare to this little man.

I looked down into his tiny face and for the first time I felt like maybe things would work out for the best. I did all I could do to please my man and make him happy, and all the while hoping he would forgive me for what I had done.

He never brought it up again, but sometimes I could see him watching me, and he'd have this look that would come across his face. He tried hard to mask it, but it showed if only for a moment.

He cared for me through my whole pregnancy and I really felt like he wanted me and the baby, but what if it all changes now that he's here. What if I have to start all over again worrying about my life?

Should I be looking over my shoulder every chance I get? I'm scared all over again. I can't be living in fear. Sometimes I think Cory would protect me, but then again I don't know.

I could hear them coming down the hall laughing and joking and it made me smile. This really feels like a real family, but how long would this all last? My room door pushed opened and in walked Isaiah and Erica, Mike and Kayle, and lastly my hubby with a big ass smile on his face. He was in heaven. It only made me feel good that I could bring that kind of joy in my baby's life.

"Hey everybody come on in?" I said as I pulled myself up in my bed. I watched as they all poured inside, but only one face held my attention. Mike's.

Mike stood in the back of the room he didn't talk or smile, and that alone is what scared me. Why couldn't anyone else see it?

"How are you feeling?" Erica asked as she reached down and gave me a hug.

"I'm tired girl, and you wouldn't believe the pain I was in."

"Oh I can guess, so when are they bringing the baby back in here?"

"They said they were going to take his vitals again and bring him right back."

"Baby do you need something?" Cory asked.

"Yes I want some water. Could you go grab me some please."

"I'll go get it." Mike said.

I laid there watching Mike's back as he left the room. In my mind I'm screaming that I don't want him to go get me shit. That nigga might try to poison me. The look I gave Cory begged him to stop Mike but he just smiled like it was all good.

Damn doesn't he see what he trying to do? Why is he letting him get me anything or do something for me at all is he crazy? Maybe this is the beginning of the pay back that they planned. I ain't drinking shit this nigga brings me.

"What's wrong with you Jamaya?" Kayla asked.

"It's nothing really why you asked?"

"You just had this strange look on your face that's all. You know I'm trained to notice those kinds of things."

"I know."

"Oh so Cory told you that I'm an FBI Agent."

"Yea he told me."

What the hell is she doing with Mike I would never understand? Before she could say anything else the nurses was rolling Lil Cory back inside the room. Every head turned and once again the attention was turned off of me.

"He's a Crawford alright." Erica said and everyone inside the room agreed.

"Mike hasn't gotten back with Jamaya water yet.I guess I'm going to have to go looking for him." Kayla said as she took one last look at the baby and walked out the room.

See that's the shit I'm talking about Cory didn't even notice that it was taking Mike so long but I did, hell even Kayla.

I watch as everyone fussed over Lil Cory and tried to relax. Man this going to be a long day.

Cory

Today was the happiest day I had in a long time. My little man came into my life full forced kicking and screaming and I loved every minute of it. My whole family is here and I feel so blessed right now. I never really believe that this day would happen, but it did and I'm thankful.

Mike surprised me when he said that "we all family now" and I hope he meant it. I wouldn't even believe that he said it if I haven't heard it with my own two ears. A baby could bring everything back together; could fix almost any problem if people let it.

I stood off to the back of the room watching everyone trying to see if anyone held any bad feeling toward Maya, but as far as I could tell I didn't see any. When I looked over at Mike and his face showed no expression at all. It was hard to read what he was thinking at that moment.

I saw that my baby was tired but she held on as long as she could. I know she needed something but water wasn't something I would have believed she would have asked for. I was hoping it was more on the lines of asking for forgiveness again.

I was happy that Mike jumped at the chance to do something nice for her, but it surprised me a little but it felt good all the same. I saw the look she gave me, but I pushed it aside because I knew she didn't believe that it's over between her and my brothers. Hell that's why I haven't said a thing in all these months.

She would learn the truth sooner or later that we are here for her and that I love her dearly. Soon she would understand that they are my family just like her and Lil Cory was.

I didn't even notice that so much time had gone pass before Kayla asked about Mike. Where the hell was he anyway? I looked over at Maya and she was looking right at me. I saw that she was scared to death.

At that moment I knew that something was going to have to change, because I can't have her afraid all the time. I walked over so I could try to calm her and hopefully this time it would make her feel safe.

"Baby are you ok?"

"Cory just go get me a bottle of water please. I don't want anything he brings back here. You see how long he's taking. I don't trust him."

"Maya you're going to have to trust him one day."

"Well it won't be today."

She gave me a weak smile and mouthed the words 'please' and I couldn't help but bend to her wishes.

"Folks I'll be right back keep an eye on my baby will you bro."

"I got ya." Isaiah said.

I walked out and headed straight to the snack machines. When I got there I didn't see Mike or Kayla anywhere. I put my dollar and twenty five cents in the machine and pushed the button for the water.

Where the hell was he he's been gone long enough to be back by now? If he didn't want to get the water for her then why did he say he was going to? This isn't making any sense at all.

When I got back inside the room I could see the relief on her face. She was glad that it was me instead of Mike. I placed the cold bottle of water in her hands and kissed her lightly on the forehead.

I'm not going to let Mike mess up my day the hell with him. I looked over at Lil Cory sleeping peacefully in Erica's arms and my heart warmed again. I don't need the drama now, because what I have is peace on earth right here and it's sleeping peacefully across the room.

As soon as I pushed Mike out my mind he came back inside the room with Kayla close behind carrying a 12 pack of bottled water and a big fruit basket. Damn I almost felt bad about thinking what I did; well almost because you'll never know with Mike.

Isaiah

No one could have been happier that this day was over with more than I was. The tension in the air so thick that you could have cut it with a knife, but everyone kept things together, and that was a good sign of healing within our family.

"I think that was a good visit don't you baby."

"Isaiah if you called that a good visit what in the hell would you call a bad one. That girl was scared out her mind when she saw Mike." Erica said and she didn't sound too happy about it.

"Erica the girl did try to have him killed."

"Yeah I know but you did say that she did try to come and work things out with him."

"I know I said that, but baby that isn't our business all right."

"I know that, but he didn't have to come in there standing there the whole time giving that girl the evil eye. Did you see her face when he said he was going to go get her water she damn near had a heart attack."

"Yeah I saw it and I bet my last dollar she isn't going to touch shit he brought her."

"Hell I wouldn't either y'all some crazy mother fucker's baby." Erica laughed.

She didn't say anything but the truth, and she knew I wouldn't have taken offence to what she just said. She's the only other person than my brothers who knew me both inside and out.

"I know baby and that's why I love you, because you know that too."

That's one of the reason why I love her the way that I do because I can be myself around her. Yeah we had our ups and downs over the years, but she's still here doing her duties and that's what's important to me, and if I'm satisfied then she damn well would be.

My phone vibrated on my hip and saw that it was Sam calling.

"Hey Sam what's up with you?"

"I'm just checking on things. I heard Jamaya had the baby today."

"Damn how the hell you heard that?"

"It doesn't take me long to hear about things that goes on in my City. I told you this once before youngin'."

I laughed because to him I'm some young boy still wet behind the ears, but I have proved myself to him over the years, so that surprised me that he still saw me that way.

"Yeah she had a little boy."

"Well a son and another killer in the family. You guys must be proud?"

"Cory is very happy."

"The whole family was there I was told."

"Man did they leave anything for me to tell you?"

"No not really, but it's nice to know that my information be on point you feel me. I have to test the waters every now and again. I just can't go taking people words of shit. Motherfuckers would love to have my ass locked up under the jail, or six feet under in a body bag."

"Sam you need to cut that shit out you no, no one in their right mind would cross you."

"But you of all people know one or two would damn show try."

"You're right and how is Sha'Maya anyway."

"My baby girl good and I can't thank you enough for your help."

"No problem."

"Tell Cory I will send a few things over for the baby as soon as I get word that they made it home."

"I got you. So are you still going to have eyes on them?"

"Yeah that not going to change."

"Why?"

"As long as you have a wolf in sheep's clothing in your family you're going to always have a problem."

Sam didn't have to say anything else on that subject. I hung up with doubt in my heart that the drama with Mike and Jamaya was far from over.

*C*hapter 13

Mike

Almost a week has passed since I last seen Cory and Jamaya. I still keep a close eye on the house waiting to see when I can get my chance to put an end to my misery. I wouldn't feel safe until she's gone and I'm a nigga that's never scared.

Even though I was miserable I got comfort in the fact that I also knew that she was too. It brought me joy to know I could put that kind of fear in her heart.

Yeah, I'm stalking my pray, and I'm doing what I'm good at. Planning my next kill.

I have dreamed of the day that I could finally make her disappear. To me it was more of a blessing when I heard her name came out of their mouths. I have planned a thousand ways for her to die, and I will continue to plan until I look in her face on that very day that she gets what she has coming.

All I do is eat, sleep, and live for the day I get my revenge. From her looks it spoke volumes to me. It told me all I needed to know. Yes she's scared. I could smell it coming out of her pours.

I'll be there for my brother when this is all over. I'll help him raise Lil Cory and soon everything would go back to normal. There's no way she could continue to walk, and the killer within me wouldn't allow it.

A week later

I know only a week has passed, but I just can't take it no more. I sat in my car waiting for Cory to fasten the baby car seat. Jamaya was going to be home along today.

My palms were sweating and that's something that I never did. I know I couldn't be feeling sorry for this bitch. My mind keeps yelling, "the baby too young to lose its mother right now", but my cold heart yelled back, "just fuck it the longer she's with the baby the harder it would be for the baby to get over losing its mother."

Cory pulled out the drive way looking only one way. I told that boy a hundred times to always take notice of your hood it's no telling who's around watching you; as you can see I'm am prime example.

I pulled out my phone and hit number 3 on my speed dial, and listened for him to pick up.

"Yo Cory what's up?"

"Shit, just was checking on things y'all need anything?"

"Naw we straight thanks for asking; where you at I just pasted your house and I didn't see your car?"

"I'm at the store that's why I was calling, but since you're good I'm going to grab a couple of things and head back home."

"Okay well if you looking for me I'm going to take the baby to his one week checkup so maybe we can stop by there when I'm finished."

"Yeah that will be good then I'll get a chance to see my nephew."

"Cool call you when I'm on my way."

Things couldn't have worked out any better. I got out the car and walked across the street. I stopped at the front door and took a look around. When I saw that things were clear I used my key and let myself inside the house. When I walked through the living room there was

Jamaya laying on the sofa asleep. I didn't try to wake her I had something else planned altogether. I walked upstairs to their bed room and pulled out a suitcase and start pulling clothes out of the closet.

I went to the dresser put in everything that she would need to look like she was leaving. I fill the suitcase and a carrying bag with as much of her things as possible.

When I got to her shoes I just toss anything in the bag. It really didn't matter she want be using them anyway. I walked back to the living room I could tell she haven't heard a sound. I walked her things back to my car and placed them in the back seat.

That didn't even take 10 minutes. I walked back to the house and was ready to put my plan into action. Today was the last day of Jamaya's life and the beginning of an end for me.

Jamaya

I don't know why but I had this funny feeling that I wasn't alone anymore. I heard something, but I know that no one's home but me. When I was about to get up I turned and looked right into Mike's face. He was sitting in a chair across from me.

"It's time to get up sleepy head; I believed you were going to sleep right through it."

"Right through what?"

"Oh come on baby girl you're not that stupid."

"Mike come one I haven't done anything else why can't you just let this go?"

"Get up."

"No I'm not getting up."

"I said get up. Don't make me come over there and get you up."

I was scared that I wouldn't move fast enough, but before I knew it he was out of that chair and pulling me to my feet. He dragged me to the front door only stopping to lock it on his way out.

"Where are you taking me Mike?"

"Just shut up bitch I don't want to hear another sound out your ugly ass mouth."

Oh my God I knew this was going to happen. I told Cory over and over again and he promised that Mike was over it. I saw it in his eyes the day I have the baby. I'm going to die today and it's nothing no one could do about it.

I watched as he drove the same route I did to the hotel I stayed in when I left Cory months ago. When he pulled to a stop in the valet section and opened the door. He gave me a look that turned my blood cold. I didn't move. I couldn't move. He walked around the car and opened up the passenger side door. I didn't wait for him to say anything I knew the drill, and I also knew this day was coming.

Once he opened the door to the lobby he looked at me. "Walk over to the desk and get the room key."

"What name am I to give them?"

"Your name fool."

"You put this room in my name?"

"Do you think I'm crazy enough to use mine? Now go and if you even look like you about to open your mouth and say something out the way I will kill you and that lovely young lady over there. You hear me?"

I knew he was telling the truth.

Yes I hear you."

I was passed scared but I knew Mike meant every word that he said. The walk seem like it took forever when it really was a few seconds. My heart was beating extra fast and my head started spinning.

"Are you alright Miss?" The lady at the receptionist day asked.

"Yes I think I have the flu thanks for asking though."

"Well ok. How my I help you?"

I looked over my shoulder and watched as Mike picked up my bags. "Yes I'm Jamaya Stevens is my room ready?"

"Let me check and see just give me a second."

I watched as she looked at the computer screen after she typed in my name.

"Yes your room is ready. Would you like some help with your bags?" She asked as she looked over at Mike.

"No thank you he got it."

I waited as she handed me my room key. As soon as she places it in my hand I realized that she's given me the same room I was in the last time I was here; room 316.

My eyes shot to Mike and he smiled. How the hell he know I stayed in that room? Could Cory have told him more then he let on.

Mike followed close behind me. I couldn't believe this was happening to me a week after having my son. The nigga couldn't even give me time with him. I never wish he was dead again not until this very moment; God he would never know how much I hate that they left him breathing.

I unlocked the room and looked around the hallway. There wasn't one person was around to witness the final moments of my life. I had no one to witness that I was last seen with Mike, well other than the lady at the front desk. When I walked inside I didn't see a need to turn around because I knew Mike was right behind me. I heard the sounds as he placed the bags on the floor and the room door close.

There was only silence in the room. Then I started to hear Mike moving around, but for the life of me I was too afraid to move. I felt as he places his ice cold hands and my shoulders. I tensed up.

I did want him touching me, but before I could say so I felt I sting in the side of my neck.

When I turned around to ask what he injected me with my vision got blurry, and my whole body started tingling all over.

"What did you just give me?"

"Just relax and let it take affect believe me your like it."

"Mike please." Was the last thing that I said as my body fell into his arms.

I could feel him lift me up and carry me to the bed.

"That's right just let it work and before long you wouldn't even remember no other feeling but this one."

I looked around but I couldn't panic. I watched he tied my feet and hands to the bed rails before my eyes slowly closed.

Cory

I couldn't wait for the baby doctor's appointment to be over with, because my mind continued to jump on Jamaya. I don't know why I feel like I should call and check on her. She has been a little down lately after the birth of the baby.

When I questioned the doctor about it he said that it was normal behavior for new mothers, and not to worry that same women have problems with depression after child birth.

The baby was in wonderful health and even gain 3 pounds since he been home. Now he's 7 pounds and 10 ounces. I couldn't help but think if her depression would affect her caring for the baby, He looked me in my eyes and said not to worry only if it looks like she is neglecting the baby or if she was trying to harm him.

To me she wasn't being as bad as that she just sleeps a lot that's all. It's normal to be tried after given birth I don't care what anyone says. She's a strong woman and she can beat that.

I guess I'll give her a little more alone time and go on and see Mike. It's been awhile since we spent some time together without the family around. I dialed his number on the way out of the doctor office.

"Hey Mike I'm just leaving here you don't mind if we still drop by there do you?"

"No I don't mind but I haven't got home yet but you can head on over there."

"What you got from the store that it took you this long?"

"Oh I been finish with that; I was doing some running around you no paying a few bills."

"Oh I was about to say if it takes you this long to shop maybe you need to let Kayla do your shopping for you."I laughed.

"Yeah yeah very funny."

"How long would it take you to get home?"

"It want be too much longer."

"Ok bro."

I picked Lil Cory up and headed for the car. I still wanted to call Maya but decided against it. The ride to our neighborhood wasn't that long. I looked in the back seat and Lil Cory was sleeping soundly.

I'm a proud parent now. It's a wonderful feeling to know that and to be able to feel complete. Hell it surprised me that I could even had these kind of feeling at all.

Isaiah

Weeks have pass and there was still no word from Jamaya. When I looked at Cory I saw the hurt on his face. I knew he was thinking that maybe this was for the best.

"You know you don't have to stay here with me anymore Isaiah." I said while reaching down to pick up the baby.

"Well to bad you're stuck with me."

"Why, I don't need know damn baby sitter."

"I didn't say that you did. All I know is that you need help with the baby, and I don't care what you have to say about it I'm staying."

I got upset, because Cory has been trying to push me away since Jamaya disappeared.

"This is my responsibility not yours. Just go home Isaiah!"

I knew he needed some alone time but he hasn't been right since they all met up at Mike's house. He needs time to heal, and I know that. What I don't understand is why want he let us help him. I think deep down he knew that Jamaya was going to run. I mean who in their right mind wouldn't.

"See now you're wrong baby brother. What you fell to see is that what's your responsibility is also mine. Okay tell me this here; if the shoe was on the other feet wouldn't you do the same thing for me?"

"You know that I would be there for you no matter what."

"Then what makes you think I wouldn't do the same thing for you huh?"

'Look Isaiah I know you're trying to help me, but I can be home by myself you know. You don't have to watch over me like I'm a little baby or something."

"So it's ok for Mike to sit here with you, but not me?"

"Mike doesn't listen to a damn thing that I have to say and you know it."

"Then why the hell would I?"

"I would hope that one of you would listen to reason and just leave me the hell alone. I can take care of my son; and I don't need y'all watching over me like I'm suicidal or something."

Once again I saw the signs that he needed some space. I know that we been crowding him, but it was something that needed to be done.

Where is she anyway? How could she just walk away from her new born baby like that? Now she has left a broken hearted killer over here that's about to explode if we don't give him the space he's asking for.

I know a losing battle when I see one so I got up and headed for the front door.

"Look Cory I'm headed over to Mike's so if you need me just call you feel me. I will be back later."

"Thank you." Cory said with a slight smile. "Now was that hard to do?"

"No my brother it wasn't, but I want to point out that I hate seeing you in pain like this."

I didn't say anymore as I walked out the door. I stopped at my car but decided not to take it because I didn't want Cory to jump in his and do a disappearing act trying to bitch us.

He just didn't understand that it took a lot of reasoning with him to make him realize that if she wanted to be found then she would be.

As I walked up Mike's driveway he was walking out the front door carrying a small carrying bag. I looked down at it and then it hit me that that wasn't the first time I saw him carrying that bag.

"Hey, where you off too?"

"I got some running around to do. What's up?"

"I just stop by that's all."

"Don't you supposed to be there with Cory?" Mike asked.

"Yeah but he needed some space. He was getting on my nerves with all that crying and shit. Hell I almost punched his ass."

"Don't feel so bad I stopped myself from doing that a time or two myself these past few weeks."

I watched Mike body language and something told me that he knew something about Jamaya whereabouts.

"Can I ask you something?"

"Yea what's on your mind?"

"What did you do to Jamaya?"

Mike stepped up into my face. "What the hell does that suppose to me?"

"Man, why you so angry I just asked a simply question?" I didn't beg down either we were eye to eye.

"I didn't do anything to the bitch how many times I have to tell y'all that."

"As many times as I have to ask to be convinced that's you didn't. I know you did something to that girl Mike, and time will tell. You know that you were wrong. You don't think that I notice when you up and disappear from time to time every day. I know you ain't with ole girl that's for damn sure."

"What you need to do Isaiah is stay the hell out my business. I said I don't know where she at and I mean it. So beg the fuck off."

Mike walked off. I watched as he threw the bag in the back seat and got inside the car and pulled off. Something inside of me was yelling for me to follow him. The only thing that stopped me was the fact that I knew I couldn't leave Cory along for too long. I don't know if it's for his safety or my peace of mind. Whatever it was it want be decided on the trip back up to Cory's house.

Chapter 14

Mike

I was pass mad as I drove back to the hotel. To be honest I had finally hit my boiling point with this whole situation. It has been weeks since I had untied Jamaya and she still want leave the hotel room. I should be happy that I got her where I want her, but it's a hollow victory because it's coming between my brothers and me.

When I walked into the hotel lobby I felt the clerk eyeing me. It didn't really matter Jamaya needed to leave here and I don't give a damn where she goes.

I used my key and entered the room. All the lights were off and the room was totally dark. The room had a stinking smell to it like she hasn't taken a bath in months.

I could hear her breathing but she wasn't making any other sounds. So I knew she wasn't dead. She had been in here for weeks now pumping her body with heroin.

It only taken me a couple of days to get her hooked and now she is like a junkie begging for a fix. I got my payback and the best part about it all is that I have her begging me to get her more. She's becoming good with injecting herself too. I don't even have to do it for her anymore.

Now she has gotten to the point that she refuse to leave the room. What she's about to learn is that this is the last supply I'm bringing her.

"Jamaya wake your ass up."

She moaned. "You got my stuff? I need it bad. I can't get out of bed."

"Yeah I got you shit. When was the last time you bath your ass man you stink like hell?"

"I don't know. Why do you even care?"

"I don't care, but you can't be walking the streets like that tomorrow Jamaya."

"What are you talking about I'm not leaving here?"

"Yes you are tonight is the last night. I did what I sat out to do."

"I hate you for this Mike!" Jamaya yelled.

"Yea, yea I know you told me that a thousand times now. Take my advice get up take a bath and for God sake eat something ain't no telling when the last time you ate a hot meal."

I walked over and turned on the light beside the bed and was shocked by what I saw, but I would never let her know that.

Once laying here was a beautiful woman and in its place is a beat up junkie.

"How am I supposed to make it without your help? You did this to me." She cried.

"You had all the time in the world to walk out this room and get help for yourself, but you choose to stay here and get high. I didn't hold a gun to your head making you continue to use that shit. You did that all by your damn self."

"You knew I was going to be hooked from that first shot, and now look at me."

"Yeah look at you." I laughed. "A sad excuse for a mother and a woman and it's all because of me."

"You must be proud of yourself?"

"A matter of a fact I'm damn proud." I laughed again the sound filling the room.

I turned back and took one last look at her and smiled. I reached inside my pocket and pulled out a hundred dollar bill and placed it on the drawer

"See you at home. I mean if you have the guts to face Cory like that."

It was the last thing I said as I closed the room.

Jamaya

It finally hit me as I watch Mike place money on the drawer that he was finished with me, but I got scared when I didn't see the drugs. I couldn't take my eyes off of it because I knew he said that he had my stuff. I jumped up fast and fell down to the floor I was weak as a baby. I used the small drawer beside the bed to pull myself up and that's when I felt my package laying there. My heart started to race as I pulled myself up off the ground.

I smiled when I saw a new needle and more heroin laying there waiting for me. My hands shake bad as I reached down to pick up what he left me. I'm in really bad shape and I know it. How could I let this get so out of hand? I reached for a half piece of a tower strap that I use to tie my arm to get a good vein. I popped my arm once and then again when my vein popped up ready to be used.

After I got hooked it was one thing that I liked about Mike was that he always have one hit fixed up and ready for me. I picked the needle up but had to stop for a second because my need was so strong. My hand was shaking and it took two tries before I was able to place it inside my arm. It didn't take long before I could feel it start to work. It was like magic because as soon as the first drop left the needle I felt myself start to fly.

I closed my eyes as my head felled back and instantly my eyes started to roll. A few seconds later my body eases down on the bed. In all of three minutes almost all the shaken had stop and I felt nothing but peace again. Will this be the only peace I feel now that I started using? It didn't take me long to realize that its hell when I don't get a hit that's the only way to explain what is happening with me.

When I came back to I still had the needle sticking out my arm. I cried like I always do when it hits me that I'm a junkie, and for the first time I smelled myself and could see what Mike was talking about.

I got up and walked into the bathroom and ran myself some bath water. My body needed a good soak. My hair needed washing and my teeth needed brushing. I don't remember the last time I did either of them. When I got to the bathroom sink and looked up in the mirror I didn't know who was standing there. It was the first time I looked at myself in weeks.

I looked horrible; tears came to me eyes once again. I looked at myself and I mean really looked at myself and I saw what I had turned into. My face had dark spots all over it and my hair was falling out when I ran my hands through it. Oh God what have I done to myself.

This is too much no wander he decided that this was the end. He set out to do what he did and made a fool out of me and he knows I could never go home and face Cory like this.

I turned around and step out of my dirty cloths and got into the streaming water. I sat there and let it ease my aching muscles as I cried. I washed my hair and put on some clean cloths, and I even called down for room service.

I knew that I couldn't eat anything heavy so a soup and salad was all I order, and when the attended arrived he smiles when he saw that I was up and dressed. It was like he was happy to see me.

"How are you doing today Ms.?"

"I'm good thank you for asking." I closed the door behind him without saying another word. I sat the food down on the table and couldn't help but think that at least somebody cares about my wellbeing.

I sat down and ate my meal like it was the first one I had in weeks. I had a million things going through my mind like where was I going to go; or would Cory let me come back home after been gone so long? I couldn't think about that anymore, because I knew I had to think about myself.

When I was done I got up all my things and put the money and drugs Mike left me inside my pocket and heading out the door.

Cory

Today went by slow, but at least I was able to be home alone again. I missed Jamaya that's for sure. It's killing me not knowing why she left us. I tried all that I could to make her happy. Even after all the crazy things she had done. I put her before my brothers and it almost messed up our relationship and still she ups and leaves me anyway. I feel like I did it all for nothing.

All I have now is our son. I placed him down inside his crib and pulled his little blanket up over him. I just finished feeding him and giving him his bath for the night. I know he would be sleep for a while I might as well try to get some sleep too.

I walked across the hall into our bedroom and the first thing I noticed was her picture on the side of the bed. God I wanted to remove it, but I know it would hurt me more if I did. No one would understand why I had to look at her pictures to make it through my days.

I undressed and headed for the shower. I didn't want to waste a lot of time you never know how long lil man was going to sleep. My mind was still working overtime as I laid there thinking that I might have to get a nanny to help out around here. I'm beginning to learn that I can't do it all on my own.

As soon as I feel asleep Jamaya smelled invaded my dreams. If was as if her perfume was surrounding me. I started to toss and turn and it had me wondering why all of a sudden her smell was so strong?

I tried to open my eyes but my mind was so sleep fogged. I started to blink my eyes so I could wake up more easily. Slowly I could see a figure sitting on the edge of the bed. I shake my head trying to push the sleep away, because I knew I couldn't be seeing Jamaya sitting on the foot of the bed.

"Baby is that you?" I asked with a voice rusty from sleep.

"It's me." Jamaya said slowly.

"Where the hell have you been?" I asked as I sat up. "This has to be a dream you couldn't be here." I said aloud.

"You're not dreaming Cory I'm here. I been here for a while"

"Where the hell have you been Maya?"

She didn't reply right off.

"It's a long story."

"I'm listening." I said as I got up out the bed walked toward the light switch.

"No leave it off." She jumped up yelling.

"Why? Baby I need to see you. I have to see that you're alright."

"I don't want you to see me like this."

"Like what? What are you talking about?"

"You're not going to want me like this Cory."

"Like what Maya? Tell me what the hell is wrong?" I reached for the light and the room lite up. "Oh my God what have you done baby?" I ran and dropped down in front her. Before I knew it I had pulled her down to the floor and into his arms.

"I told you baby. I'm sorry."

"Maya what happen please tell me?"

My heart had broken into a million pieces as I looked at the love of my life. I saw how she had wasted away.

"I messed up everything and now I have to make things right for you."

"You're talking crazy."

"I know it might sound that way, but it's true."

"What are you on?"

"Does it matter?"

"Hell yea it matters. We can get you some help baby. Please let me help you."

"There's no help for me Cory." Maya said as she cried and placed her head on my shoulder. "I want something to drink. Can you go get me some water?"

"I don't want to leave you?"

"I'm not going anywhere."

"You promise?" I looked at her and watched as another tear fell from her eyes.

"I promise. I will be here when you get back."

"Ok be back in a second baby. Its ok don't worry I will take care of you."

She smiled a teary smile and I saw that she was saddened by the choices she had made by getting on drugs. The trip to the kitchen only took a couple of minutes. When I walked back inside the bedroom Maya was laid out on the floor with a needle stuck inside her arm. Her eyes were staring up at the ceiling and her mouth was covered with white foam.

My heart stopped as I looked at her lying half dead on the floor. I dropped to my knees and lifted her head up into my arms. All I could do was hold her still shaking body close to me.

"Why baby? Why did you do this? I told you I would help you."

I knew there wasn't anything left for me to do for her so I held her close and continued to tell her that I loved her. I kissed her softly on the forehead as she took her last breath.

Isaiah

I couldn't believe what I was hearing as I listen to Sam talk on the other end of the phone. Why haven't I called him weeks again.

"Sam if you knew all of this was happening why didn't you tell me?"

"It wasn't my place to tell you. If you would have come to me when she first disappeared I would have told you where she was, but you didn't do that until now."

"Damn Sam I didn't think of it until I remembered that you said you had somebody watching us. That's was the first thing I did was call you."

"What made you call and ask me tonight?"

"Something was eating at me about Mike. I had a feeling that he had something to do with her disappearance. I should have known because my feelings were never wrong when it came to my brothers. I just hate that I'm right."

"Isaiah you know I'm down with you boys, you're like family, but don't be too hard on Mike he had to do what he had to do."

"That's understandable but···"

"There's no but Isaiah that girl tried to have him killed twice, and that's just not acceptable. I know you love your brother, but please don't let that selfish little bitch come in between y'all."

"So what should I do act like I don't know?"

"Yea that's what I'm saying Isaiah. Hold on a minute will you."

I sat there thinking while I was waiting for Sam to come back on the line. He was right. I knew it. I just refuse to believe that he had anything to do with

Jamaya disappearing, and not say one thing to me. Why would he do something like this on his own? I know he had revenge in his heart, but this here.

Would it be easier for me to act like I know nothing? Could I look in my brother's face day after day seeing him break down slowly over the loss of his girl? Would I be able to handle that kind of pressure?

"Ok I'm back." Sam said cutting into my thoughts. "Just chill Isaiah and anything will work itself out."

"Well at least I know where she's at now. Thank you for the information Sam."

"No problem son just hit me up if you need anything else, and Isaiah next time don't wait so long to contact me you hear me."

"You got it Sam." Before I could even get that out my other line beeped. "Hey why you calling so late?"

"It's Maya she came back home tonight?" Cory cried into the phone.

"Cory what's wrong?"

"She's dead man."

"Who's dead Maya?"

I could hardly hear him over the crying of the baby.

"Yes Maya."

"I'm on my way."

I hang up, but I had to catch myself before I called Mike. I needed to wait and see what happened before I made that phone call, but knowing Cory he might already have.

I pulled up in front of Cory's house and the police and paramedics were already on the scene. Jumping out the truck I ran toward the front door and was stopped by the police.

"Sir you not allowed in there." One of officers stated as he reached his hand out to stop me.

"It's ok that's my brother." Cory said to the officer.

When I reached him he handed the baby over to me and walked off. I followed close behind, and when we got to the kitchen Cory started warming the baby up a bottle.

"Why didn't you call me before you called the police?"

"Why I ain't got nothing to hide."

"I know that, but still you don't need those pigs all up in your shit like this. Look at this." I pointed. "They're all over the fucking place."

"It's all good. Did you call Mike?"

"No I was about to ask you the same thing. Is she still in the house?"

"Yeah, she's upstairs in the bedroom."

"I'm going up to make sure everything is going smoothly."

"No, I don't want you seeing her like that."

"Seeing her like what? What the hell happened to her, and how she got here in the first place?"

"She died of an overdose, and I don't know how she got here to be honest. I just woke up and she was sitting on the foot of the bed."

"What?"

"That's what I'm saying. I believed I was dreaming at first, but I smelled her perfume, and I knew I couldn't be. Isaiah man she was so scared, and I wanted to help her. I begged her to let me help her."

"What did she say? Where was she all this time?"

"She wouldn't tell me." Cory broke down again. "She sent me to the kitchen to get her some water and when I came back she was lying there damn near scared me to death."

"Man I knew I shouldn't have left you here along."

"Don't you see maybe that's way she took so long to come back because y'all were always here?"

"I don't think so Cory. The way you telling things it sounds like she was far gone man."

"I could have helped her."

"I know you could have, but maybe this is for the best."

"How is this for the best when she left me and our baby huh you tell me that?"

"I don't know Cory I'm going to call Mike now and let him know what's going on."

I pulled my phone out my pocket as I gave him back the baby and walked out the house. But instead of calling Mike I called Sam again.

Sam didn't even say hello when he answered the phone. "So now you see why I said what I did?" Sam asked into the phone.

"Once again you knew she was dead and you didn't say a damn a thing."

"I told you to chill and it will all play itself out and it has am I right?"

"Yeah it did, and I don't see a reason to let anyone of them know that I knew anything about what happened to her. Sam I don't know if I could just drop it but I will try my best to let this go."

"That's what I been trying to tell you."

"I got you."

I knew that there wasn't anything else left to say to Sam. He's always right and a very wise man. He wouldn't have gotten to where he's at by doing crazy shit. I kept that in mind as I placed my next call.

Mike

When I received the phone call from Isaiah it shocked me to the core. I never expected her to really go home, and on top of that overdose in their house. I got out of bed and got dressed. I looked at the empty spot where Kayle usually slept before I left the house. I didn't even find it necessary to waste gas going up there. A walk would do me good on this special day I said to myself with a smile on my face.

When I reached the house I saw cop cars were everywhere, there was crime scene tape going all around the house. I walked up and stopped in front of the house, and that's when I saw Isaiah jump out of his truck and head in my direction. Before he made it half way

Jamaya's body was being wheeled out the house.

We stood side by side and looked on as they placed her inside the van and rode away.

"You damn sure took your time coming up here." Isaiah said a little too sharply.

"Sorry I was in the bed had to get dressed. So how is Cory?"

"Not so good, but I gave him some time alone. When I left out to call you he was feeding the baby."

"So she came home huh. Did she tell him where she been?" I had to ask.

I had to find out if Cory knew anything about how she ended up that way. When I looked at Isaiah I saw something in his eyes. It only showed for a second or maybe I'm just seeing things, but I could tell he wanted to say something. If he knows anything he damn show isn't talking.

"No, she wouldn't tell him anything, and I wonder why that is?"

"Who knows what been going through that girls mind."

I didn't say anything else just headed for the house I needed to find out if Jamaya said anything to Cory? This wasn't my plan. I didn't think she had it in her to come back here. Damn maybe that was a mistake to let her walk. I don't want her breaking my family apart. We are all we have there's no one else left.

"If you are looking for your brother he's upstairs."

"Thanks officer. Are you about finished here now?"

"Yes we just finished wrapping things up and you are sir?"

"Oh I'm sorry I'm Mike Cory's oldest brother." I said as I took his hand in a firm handshake.

"Well Mike the house is all yours again and we will remove all the tape before we leave. Once again we are sorry for your loss." Officer Holloway said on his way out the front door.

"I never thought I see the day that I be shaking hands with a cop and not sitting on the other side of one of the tables." I said laughing.

"I know right. I think it's a first time for everything."

When we made it up stairs Cory was sitting on the foot of his bed with his head in his hands. I felt sorry for him. I really did. I hate that she came here and did this in front of him.

"Cory I'm going to go pack the baby a few things Erica and I are going to watch him for a few days so you can get yourself together so you can make the arrangements for Jamaya."Isaiah said as he sat down beside Cory. He put his hand on his shoulder and gave it a light squeeze.

"Thank you Isaiah and please tell Erica I appreciate this very much."

"I think you need to stay at my place the rest of the night Cory." I said but the look he gave me stopped me in mid-sentence. "Is something wrong bro?"

How the hell could you ask me that Mike as you can see my baby is laying cold in some damn freezer right now? So yes I will say that something is wrong." Cory yelled and jumped to his feet.

I stepped back I didn't know where this was heading. "I know that Cory and I am sorry."

"Are you really?"

"You know that I am. Where is all this coming from?"

Cory laughed. "I can't believe you're standing here acting like you really care that she's dead."

"What the hell does that supposed to mean."

"Maya always said that you will never forgive her. She couldn't let it go that you will still be out to get her. I tried all I could to make her feel safe, but nothing I ever did was good enough for her."

"Where are you going with all of this?" Isaiah asked once he was up and on his feet too. I want to blame you Mike I really do. "Cory stepped up closer in my face.

"Why?"

I was praying that she didn't say anything to him but I see now that she may have.

"You always knew that she was afraid of you. Even after she came to you and asked for forgiveness you still held hatred in your heart for her, and she knew that."

"Damn Cory what was is it that you wanted from me?" I asked him and I couldn't help but let all my pain show. "You wanted me to act like it didn't happen? You weren't the one that had to learn how to walk again. You weren't the one that woke up night after night from nightmares. I was. You aren't the one who still feels like you have to watch over your shoulder all the time. I am. I don't have eyes in the back on my head."

I know that. Just like I know I couldn't expect you to forgive her, but you could at least ease her mind just a little bit."

"I'm not going to stand here and lie to you saying that it doesn't please me that she is dead, but it saddens me. All because I know that you are hurting because of it."

It's been a long time since I pulled my brother in my arms for a hug but right now I believed we were all in need of one. So I held him close just like I use to do when he was younger.

Yes it hurts me to know that I'm part of the reason he is feeling this pain. It also hurts me that he would have to raise his son up on his own, but that's what we are here for. We're family and no one or nothing would come in between that.

Gangsta Killers

New

Releases

Love or Death: I closed my eyes and tried to sleep. The nightmares kept creeping in. He was hitting me with relentless force. He wouldn't stop. Would I live through this? Christina "Wada" Thomas thought she had met the perfect vato when she met Marco, little did she know that her knight would take her on a dark and twisted road of drug abuse. The final showdown being when he tried to get her into prostitution. We take a journey through Weda's Vida Loca and the climax being when she lives through The Day of the Dead or does she? Did her path lead to Love or Death?

The Hitman's Dauther's: The Hitman's Daughters tell a story of many interesting people living in the streets of Atlanta, GA. Many hard times, family secrets, stuggles, and troubles center one of the main characters, Star. Join us as we all learn more about Star, Muffin, Red. Tracey, Stacy, Rick, and Tony as they battle this life.

This is E book only···

http://www.snackphood.com/store/product.php?id_product=34

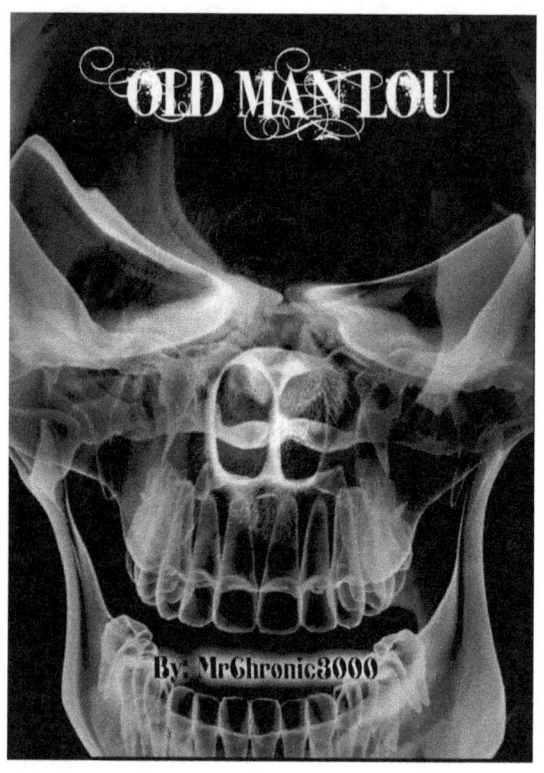

Lou was a well-known figure in his neighborhood. He had everything going for him. Then one day news spreads of Lou's suicide. He allegedly shot his self with a .38.Only problem is Lou didn't own a .38. Detective Danny Westfield was Lou's young protégé and husband to Lou's daughter. One day Danny gets word that Lou's Death was not a suicide. Det. Westfield begins a journey for answers. The more he digs the more he finds out that this case is bigger than Lou. No one can be trusted. Everyone is a suspect. Join Det. Westfield on his journey for answers.

WBP&TLF
Presents

PEEK-A-BOO

"THE SAFETY DEPOSIT BOX"

Written By:
Veronica Meek
Mike Sudler

Greg has an eye on his neighbor who happens to cross his path in his very near future. When Susan first met him she felt a familiar presence about him, like they met before. When the sparks fly, the meeting of the two is more than spectacular... It's blissful. But while love is in the air, so are the bullets and bodies are dropping all around them.

Nisha's Black Publications PRESENTS

Aaliyah's Secret

Nikki B

Aaliyah has a secret that could change her life forever. It puts two brothers "Sam and Charles's against one another. Will the steps Aaliyah takes to cover up her secret be worth it?

Coming

Soon

Justified Means To The End: The everyday complex struggles of Mik'hail Drayton. An inner city youth raised in the cold streets of Savannah, GA criminal underworld as a product of his environment.

Through his trials and tribulations he takes an oath to uplift his people and learns the truth about "Freedom of Choice". In the game of life and death, he learns that stakes are high and bets are eternal. Mik'hail must choose between his free-will and will to be free. Either way he must learn that those who master the game know and understand that only the End can Justify the Means